Dear Reader

Georgie and Josh lived in my imagination for close to a year before I had a chance to begin their story. I thought it would be easy because I knew them so well by this time. I was wrong! (Please keep that to yourself as it's something my husband would love to hear me admit!)

This story was a battle of wills: mine versus my characters. Almost always my characters take on their own very distinct personalities, but I usually still feel that I am in control of their story. Not this time! Georgie and Josh refused to behave. But they're like my kids—I still love them even if they're misbehaving, and I do like it when they show a bit of spirit.

So eventually, with much angst on my part and much rebellion on their part, we found a way to compromise. They might have tested my patience but I was very pleased ultimately to give them the happiness they deserved.

I hope you love Georgie and Josh as much as I did.

Best wishes

Emily

GEORGIE'S BIG GREEK WEDDING?

BY
EMILY FORBES

First published in Great Britain 2012
by Mills & Boon, an imprint of Harlequin (UK) Limited.
Harlequin (UK) Limited, Eton House, 18-24 Paradise Road,
Richmond, Surrey TW9 1SR

ISBN: 978 0 263 22867 0

Harlequin (UK) policy is to use papers that are natural, renewable
and recyclable products and made from wood grown in sustainable
forests. The logging and manufacturing process conform to the
legal environmental regulations of the country of origin.

Printed and bound in Great Britain
by CPI Antony Rowe, Chippenham, Wiltshire

Emily Forbes began her writing life as a partnership between two sisters who are both passionate bibliophiles. As a team Emily had ten books published, and one of her proudest moments was when her tenth book was nominated for the 2010 Australian Romantic Book of the Year Award.

While Emily's love of writing remains as strong as ever, the demands of life with young families has recently made it difficult to work on stories together. But rather than give up her dream Emily now writes solo. The challenges may be different but the reward of having a book published is still as sweet as ever.

Whether as a team or as an individual Emily hopes to keep bringing stories to her readers. Her inspiration comes from everywhere, and stories she hears while travelling, at mothers' lunches, in the media and in her other career as a physiotherapist all get embellished with a large dose of imagination until they develop a life of their own.

If you would like to get in touch with Emily you can e-mail her at emilyforbes@internode.on.net, and she can also be found blogging at the Harlequin Medical Romance blog: www.harlequin.com

CHAPTER ONE

Josh swung himself out of the ocean and onto the back of the pontoon. Slipping his dive fins from his feet and his mask from his face, he held them in one hand as he used his free hand to haul himself into a standing position. The air tank on his back was ungainly, making his balance awkward, but he was used to the sensation and after more than two hundred dives he knew better than to try to lean forward while changing position.

He dropped his fins, mask and snorkel into his dive bag and checked his watch, noting the dive time and depth. It had been a fairly standard dive, pleasant but certainly not the best. The visibility had been reasonable but aside from a few eels and one huge Maori wrasse he hadn't seen anything spectacular.

He was disappointed. He'd hoped the easy access to the world-renowned Great Barrier Reef dive sites off the coast of Cairns in northern Queensland would make up for the fact he'd had to transfer to this country town. He unclipped his buoyancy vest and slung it from his back. Okay, to be fair, Cairns was a large regional centre, not a typical Australian country town, but it definitely wasn't a big city. He'd spent the past two and a half years in Brisbane, a city of two million people, working his way up to a senior position, or so he'd thought, only to find himself banished to the sticks for six months.

But he'd survived smaller towns before, much smaller, all for the sake of experience, and he just hoped this move would pay dividends too. Besides, it wasn't like he'd had much of a choice. His six-month stint started tomorrow and he'd have to make the most of it.

He would take the opportunity to have one last holiday before he prepared to knuckle down and work hard to achieve the goals he'd set himself. He would be free to do as he pleased on his days off but once he returned to Brisbane he imagined days off would be few and far between.

Have fun, he told himself as he pulled his thin dive shirt over his head before running his hands through his hair to dry it off, but remember to think of the bigger picture and of what you stand to gain, that was the way to get through the next six months.

Georgie pushed herself out of the warm water and onto the ledge at the back of the pontoon that was moored permanently at Agincourt Reef. She removed her mask and snorkel as she dangled her legs in the ocean and watched the myriad holidaymakers splashing around, enjoying the beauty of the reef.

Her stomach rumbled as she basked in the afternoon sunshine, reminding her that she'd skipped lunch in favour of a longer snorkel. She pulled the flippers from her feet so she could stand and threw her borrowed diving equipment into the containers at the back of the pontoon. The deck was almost deserted now that most of the day-trippers had consumed their lunches and returned to the water, so she'd go and see what remained of the buffet.

She hung her life jacket on the rack and let her eyes

roam over the handful of people gathered on the pontoon. Her gaze lingered on the starboard side where a group of scuba divers had just emerged from the water and were now laboriously removing their equipment. She searched the group for her brother Stephen and his girlfriend, Anna, who were visiting from Melbourne and had come out to the reef to go scuba diving, but she didn't see any familiar faces. They must still be in the water.

They'd tried to talk her into doing an introductory dive and initially she'd been keen, but she'd chickened out when they'd reached the pontoon and she'd seen the huge expanse of empty ocean. Who knew what was lurking under there? She decided she felt safer splashing about with all the other snorkellers. Being able to lift her head out of the water and see the pontoon and the catamarans that had ferried them to the reef gave her a sense of security out in the middle of the vast Pacific Ocean.

She continued to watch the group of divers, smiling at their attempts to shed their equipment. They'd looked so graceful under the water when she'd seen them from her snorkelling vantage point but out of it they looked ungainly. She was glad she'd changed her mind about the introductory dive—she wasn't sure she could be bothered with all the paraphernalia and the air tanks looked awfully heavy.

There was one man, however, who managed to make the tank look as though it weighed no more than a sleeping bag. Georgie watched as he unclipped his buoyancy vest and slung it and his air tank off his shoulders before he removed his thin dive shirt by pulling it over his head. His torso was bare and she was treated to a rather attractive view of a smooth, lightly tanned back and rippling muscles as he stretched his arms overhead. His dark blond hair was cut short and when he ran his hands through it the salt water made it stick up in all directions. He had the physique of a man who worked out. He had broad, square shoulders that tapered nicely into his waist and the muscles on his arms were well defined.

He threw his shirt over his shoulder as her eyes travelled down his back. She could see the two small dimples at the base of his spine just visible above the waistband of his shorts. His shorts hugged the curve of his buttocks and were patterned like the Australian flag. If all divers looked like him, perhaps she would take up the challenge.

'Help, somebody, please, help us.'

Georgie spun around, her meandering thoughts interrupted by a woman's cries. The sound came from her right, out in the ocean. She searched the water and it took her a second or two to locate the woman. She was about fifty metres off the back of the pontoon in one of the snorkelling areas marked out by floating buoys. The woman was waving one arm and hanging onto someone else with her other hand. From the corner of her eye Georgie saw a flash of movement as someone dived off the starboard corner of the pontoon. She turned her head. The guy in the Australian flag board shorts had disappeared. In the time it took her to process the cries for help and to find the source of the sound he had dived into the water and was now swimming strongly towards the distressed woman.

A couple of crew members had raced to the back of the pontoon, one unhooking a lifebuoy and the other carrying a first-aid kit. Seeing other people in action galvanised Georgie. She made her way across the pontoon, past stunned tourists, to offer her assistance as the crewman with the lifebuoy jumped overboard and struck out towards the woman, trailing in the other guy's wake.

Georgie followed him with her eyes. She could see that the diver in the Aussie flag shorts had almost reached the woman but it was getting difficult to see everything that was happening as the swell had picked up and the small waves breaking on the top of the reef were obscuring her vision. With two more over arm strokes, the guy in the board shorts had reached the woman and taken over control of the person she was supporting. He had hold of the person's chin and Georgie could see him making his way back to the pontoon with a strong sidestroke action, dragging the person with him. The woman was doing her best to follow but she was being rapidly left behind. The crewman with the lifebuoy swam up to her, slipped the lifebuoy over her head and under her arms and started towing her back to the pontoon.

The guy in the board shorts was already back at the pontoon with the rescued man in his grip. One of the crewmen knelt down at the edge of the pontoon and hooked his hands under the distressed man's armpits and hauled him onto the deck.

'He's complaining of chest pain,' the diver in the board shorts told the crewman as he helped to lift the man's legs out of the water, 'and I suspect he's aspirated some salt water.'

What sort of person used the term 'aspirated'? Georgie wondered. It was a medical term but perhaps it was common in diving as well? She watched the diver as he hoisted himself up onto the deck. His biceps and triceps bulged as he lifted his weight clear of the sea. Salt water streamed from his body as he stood. His chest was smooth and tanned and despite having just swum a fast fifty metres while towing a heavy body, he was breathing normally. He didn't appear to be even slightly out of breath.

There were now several people gathered around the back of the pontoon and Georgie was able to blend into the crowd. The guy seemed oblivious to her scrutiny so she let her gaze travel higher.

She was pleased to see that he had a face to match his body. He had an oval face with strong features that complemented his chiselled physique. He had full lips set above a firm jaw, which had a day's growth of beard and perfectly symmetrical, sandy brown eyebrows that framed his eyes. His nose was straight and narrow and his teeth, when he spoke, were even and white. He was rather cute.

'Let's clear the area and get him comfortable. We don't want to encourage extra blood flow to his heart. I don't want to stress it more than necessary.'

The cute guy, as Georgie now thought of him, continued to issue instructions as he directed the crew to reposition the man where he wanted him. Because of the board shorts he was wearing she'd initially wondered if he was an overseas tourist but he spoke with a definite Aussie twang. Foreign or not, the cute guy was sounding more and more like he had a medical background. Which reminded her of why she'd crossed the deck in the first place. It hadn't been to ogle a complete stranger, she'd meant to offer assistance. There were more important things to focus on than an attractive scuba diver.

She took a couple of steps away from the cute guy and towards the crew member who was standing nearby, holding the first-aid kit.

'Have you got a towel or something we can use to dry him off and keep him warm?' she asked.

He nodded and Georgie took the kit from him so he could go and find what she'd asked for. She squatted down and spoke to the cute guy. 'I'm a paramedic. Can I help?'

He nodded in acknowledgement but kept his head down and directed his words at the patient. 'I'm a doctor so between us we should be able to get you sorted.' For a moment Georgie thought he was going to ignore her but when he finished reassuring the patient he looked across at her.

His eyes were an unusual shade of grey. Silvery grey, almost metallic in colour, they reminded her of the paint the Navy used on its ships. 'Can you have a look and see what's in the first-aid kit?' he asked.

She flipped the catches open as she listened to the conversation going on beside her.

'Can you describe your pain to me?'

'I feel like someone has punched me in the chest.' The man spoke with a British accent and he sounded out of breath, as though each word took great effort. He was going to have a holiday to remember, Georgie thought, assuming they managed to pull him through this crisis.

'Have you had chest pain before?' Cute guy had his fingers on the man's wrist pulse and his eyes on his dive watch, counting the seconds. His fingers were long and slender, his nails shortly clipped and nicely shaped.

The patient nodded but the woman, whom Georgie assumed was his wife, and who was now back on board the pontoon thanks to the efforts of the crew member, elaborated. 'His doctor said it was angina.'

'Is he on any medication?' Cute guy quizzed the man's wife.

Georgie made a concerted effort to turn her attention back to the contents of the first-aid kit and away from the cute doctor's hands.

'The doctor gave Nigel some tablets.'

'Have you got them with you?'

The wife shook her head. 'We forgot to pack them—they're in our hotel room.'

Fat lot of good they were going to do there, Georgie thought. She looked up from the first-aid kit and caught cute guy's eye. It was obvious from his expression he was thinking along the same lines.

'There's nothing useful in here,' she muttered as she

finished searching through the kit. The crewman had returned with a towel but Georgie had another assignment for him now. 'Do you have a medical cupboard that would have any drugs other than mild analgesics? Painkillers,' she clarified, when all she got was a blank look.

He nodded. 'Yes, we've got a sick bay. If you want to come with me, you can see if we've got what you need.'

Georgie stood and quickly followed him along the deck into the small sick room. She grabbed a portable oxygen cylinder that was hooked up against the wall as the crewman unlocked a medicine cupboard. She hunted through the cupboard and found some GTN spray and a mask to use with the oxygen. There wasn't much else that was helpful.

She returned to the back of the pontoon with her meagre supplies. 'Symptoms?' she queried, wanting to know whether the patient's status had changed.

'Pulse rate irregular and possibly slightly elevated,' cute guy said as she squatted beside him. He smelt of salt and sunshine and Georgie could feel the heat of the sun bouncing off him. 'Shortness of breath,' he continued speaking, 'but that could be exercise related. Left-sided chest pain but not extending into his extremities.' He turned to look at her and the movement made his abdominals ripple along his side.

'How long since his symptoms started?' she asked, forcing herself to concentrate.

He glanced at his watch. 'We've been out of the water for four and a half minutes and his pain's no worse.'

'Angina?' she queried.

He nodded in agreement. 'Most probably.'

'I found this.' Georgie held up the spray. 'I think it's our best option.' She expected the doctor to move over and let her administer the spray but he reached out and took it

from her. She was a little bit taken aback. She had no idea
what sort of doctor this man was but, as a paramedic, she
was almost certain she'd have more experience in these
situations than him and she wasn't used to playing second
fiddle. But she wasn't going to have an argument about
it—after all, it was a fairly simple exercise and he'd already
given Nigel the spray. All that was left was to monitor him
and hope his condition improved.

Georgie saw Nigel's wife waiting anxiously nearby. She
swallowed her irritation. Someone needed to talk to the
wife. 'I'll call QMERT and put them on alert but hopefully
we'll get him stabilised,' she told the doctor as she stood
up. 'And I'll explain what's happening to his wife.'

To save time she spoke to a crew member and Nigel's
wife together so she only had to explain things once.
'Nigel's symptoms aren't worsening so hopefully it's just
a case of angina,' she told them. 'He's been given medication and we'll monitor him for the next ten minutes. If it
is angina, we expect his symptoms will have eased con-
siderably in that time.'

'And if they don't? What do we do then?' Nigel's wife
asked. 'We're out in the middle of the ocean.'

'I'm going to radio QMERT, that's the Queensland
Medical Emergency Retrieval Team.' Georgie kept her
voice calm as she wanted to stem the rising panic she could
hear in the wife's voice. 'I'll explain the situation and get
a helicopter on standby to evacuate him if necessary.' She
didn't mention that she worked with QMERT, it wouldn't
make any difference to anyone else.

Georgie got a few more details from Nigel's wife and
put a call in to the Clinical Coordination centre in Brisbane
to advise them of the situation. All calls to QMERT went
through Brisbane. It was up to the central command to
find the closest available crew from one of the bases lo-

cated throughout Queensland. It was more than likely that Cairns, which was her base, or the Townsville crew would be put on standby.

She finished the call and returned to the patient. The cute doctor looked up at her with his gunship-grey eyes and Georgie forgot she was annoyed at him.

'He's recovering well, chest pain abating and respirations normal.'

'So you think we're okay to bring him in on the boat?' Georgie asked.

'How long will that take?'

Georgie frowned. Had she misheard him? Hadn't he come out to the reef on the boat? Was his cool grey gaze interfering with her concentration?

'About ninety minutes,' she replied, 'but it's not due to leave for another hour. There's time to alter plans if things change. I've put the QMERT chopper on standby.'

He stood up. 'Can I speak to you over here?' he asked, inclining his head towards the side railing of the pontoon.

Georgie wondered what he couldn't say in front of Nigel and his wife but she nodded anyway. He held out a hand. She reached for him and he clasped his fingers around her wrist to help her to her feet, but when his skin met hers a spark shot through her. It made her catch her breath. It made her heart race. It must have something to do with the adrenaline coursing through her system after the excitement, she thought. He let go of her hand and walked over to the edge of the pontoon, away from Nigel, his wife and the crewman, who was still hovering waiting for any further instructions. Georgie followed him, she didn't think she could do anything else. Her feet seemed to be behaving independently of her brain, following his lead.

He leant on the railing and Georgie could see each bony

prominence of his vertebrae where his spine curved as he bent forward.

'Are you happy to monitor him and make that call if necessary?'

Her frown deepened. 'Of course.' She had no problem with that but she wondered why he was handing total patient care over to her.

'I flew out to the reef on a helicopter charter,' he explained, 'and I've just been told it needs to take off as there's another chopper coming in onto the landing pontoon shortly. But I can stay to help monitor Nigel if you like. I need to know what you're comfortable with before I tell him what's happening. I could come back on the catamaran with you if you'd prefer.'

Did he think she couldn't handle things? Was that why he'd offered? He didn't need to do her any favours.

'Thank you but I can manage. I'm used to working in these conditions,' she said as she looked around the pontoon and the expanse of water surrounding it. 'Well, perhaps not these exact conditions, but I'm certainly used to coping outside a hospital environment. If I'm at all concerned I'll call QMERT in. They can do an evacuation from the catamaran if things get really dicey. It's fine. Go.'

Go and let me concentrate. She knew it would be better if she was left to work on her own. After all, she'd wanted to be in charge.

There was a stretcher fixed alongside the stairs that led to the upper deck, and she instructed the crew to bring it to her as she swapped places with the doctor. She watched him as he gathered his things and boarded the little dinghy that would ferry him across to the helicopter pontoon.

She watched him as he left her to monitor Nigel. That wasn't an issue. She was more than capable. She didn't need his help. She could work more efficiently without the distraction. But as the dinghy pulled away from the pontoon, she wondered where he was from and, as he raised a hand in farewell, she realised she had no way of finding out. She didn't even know his name.

CHAPTER TWO

GEORGIE parked her car beside the airport building that was the headquarters for the Cairns division of QMERT. She climbed out and pulled her white singlet top away from her body, looking for some respite from the heat. A quarter to eight in the morning and the north Queensland humidity was already stifling. She could feel the perspiration gathering between her breasts. She'd been in the tropics for months now but after moving from the cooler climes of Melbourne she still hadn't got used to feeling hot and sticky ninety per cent of the time. But despite the sometimes intolerable humidity she was thoroughly enjoying her secondment to the Queensland Ambulance Service and QMERT.

And the weather wasn't always so oppressive, she reminded herself. It had been remarkably pleasant out on the reef yesterday. It was only on the mainland that she noticed the humidity. The scenery yesterday had been very pleasant too, she recalled with a smile. It had been a pity the cute doctor had left before she'd got his name.

She still hadn't decided whether she was more annoyed or intrigued by him. She had to give him credit for his quick reaction to the crisis yesterday. Nigel had made it safely back to the Cairns hospital and he had the doctor to thank for that. She supposed he'd only been doing what he'd been trained for and she couldn't hold that against him. But, still, she wished she knew who he was.

She'd kept her eyes peeled last night when she'd gone out to dinner with her brother and sister-in-law, hoping she might see him wandering the streets of Cairns, but her search had been fruitless. She shrugged. She'd expected nothing less really, it had been a rather vain hope. But it had been her only hope. The only way she might see him again. More than likely he was just a tourist, just someone passing through Cairns, someone she was never likely to see again. But that idea was strangely disappointing.

She shook her head, trying to clear it. She had other things to think about than a perfect stranger. It was time to go to work. She searched through her bag for an elastic band to tie up her hair. The air was muggy, heavy with moisture, and having her hair hanging halfway down her back was making her feel hotter. She gathered her dark hair into a ponytail that hung in a thick rope between her shoulder blades, picked up her bag and headed for the air-conditioned comfort of the corrugated-iron and weatherboard building.

She walked past the helicopter that was the latest addition to the QMERT fleet. The night crew was obviously back at base and she wondered what kind of shift they'd had. She hummed show tunes as she crossed the tarmac, pushed open the door to the base and headed for the communications centre. Comms was always her first port of call as she always wanted to check what was happening.

'Morning, Lou, what have I missed?' she greeted the dispatch officer who was stationed at her desk.

'Nothing much,' was the answer. 'The boys have just got back from an IHT,' Louise went on, using the abbreviation for an inter-hospital transfer, 'but other than that it was pretty quiet overnight.'

Georgie pulled a face, her dark eyes flashing with good humour. She loved the pace and hype of busy days. Flying off in the helicopter to save lives was a huge buzz and while quiet days were good because they meant no one was getting injured, busy days meant the chance to put her skills to use.

'It's not all bad,' Louise added. She knew how Georgie felt about quiet days—everyone on the team felt the same. 'The new doctor starts officially today. Showing him the ropes should keep you out of trouble.'

'That's Josh Wetherly, right? The emergency specialist from Brisbane?' Georgie recalled some details from the bio that had been circulating about him.

Louise nodded. 'His experience looks pretty good on paper but, trust me, he looks even better in real life. I reckon you'll be more than happy to show him around the chopper and maybe even around Cairns.'

Georgie rolled her eyes. She was used to Louise trying to find her a man. Louise and her husband had been married for twenty-five years and she thought everyone deserved the same happiness. Georgie didn't disagree. Her parents were also a fine example of a happy marriage, but she didn't want to be reminded that at twenty-seven years of age people were starting to expect her to settle down. There were still things she wanted to do before she settled down to domestic life and she certainly didn't need another mother figure trying to find her a husband. Her own mother was perfectly capable of that! Besides, at fifty and almost twice her age, Louise's idea of a hot man was not quite the same as Georgie's. It took more than good manners and a nice head of hair to get her attention.

One of the reasons Georgie had moved to Cairns had been to get away from the pressure her family had been putting on her to find a partner but so far her plan wasn't working too well. Her family continued to show a tendency to send eligible bachelors her way and she'd lost count of the number of blind dates she'd been obliged to go on. She didn't need Lou on her case as well. She needed a project, something to occupy her time so she could legitimately say she was too busy to date. Showing Dr Wetherly around Cairns wasn't her idea of a suitable project. She'd have to find something else.

The phone on Louise's desk rang before Georgie could think of a smart retort. She waited for Lou to take the call, knowing it would probably mean a job for the team.

Lou jotted notes as she spoke to the clinical co-ordinator in Brisbane, nearly fourteen hundred kilometres south of their Cairns base. The information the retrieval team received was almost always third hand: the emergency call would be put through to headquarters in Brisbane and, depending on the location of the emergency, the Brisbane co-ordinator would pass the call on to the dispatch clerk in Brisbane, Townsville, Toowoomba or Cairns. They would then pass the information on to the retrieval team. QMERT was responsible for an area extending in a radius a few hundred kilometres around Cairns, including the waters and islands in the Pacific Ocean off the coast of Australia. The Royal Flying Doctor Service took over to the north up to Cape York and further inland into the Outback, while QMERT Townsville covered the area to the south.

Louise hung up the phone and relayed the scant information she had to Georgie. 'A four-month-old baby in respiratory distress. She's in Tully hospital, they've requested an IHT. I'll find Pat—'

'And I'll get changed and track down Dr Wetherly.' Georgie finished Lou's sentence. She knew she had time. Pat, the helicopter pilot on duty, would need to get details about the flight and landing, do his pre-flight checks and refuel if necessary. She only needed a few minutes to get changed and find the new doctor. A job this early in the morning wasn't going to be an ideal introduction for the new recruit on his first day but there was no way around it. She just hoped he was up to the challenge.

She headed for the change rooms to stow her bag and change into the navy and grey jumpsuit that was the retrieval team's uniform. As she pushed open the door and stepped around the privacy wall that screened the room from the corridor she was greeted by the sight of semi-naked men. The QMERT building was not overly large and the change rooms were unisex. There was a central changing area divided by lockers with male and female showers and toilets off to each side, which afforded a little privacy but not a lot.

The night-shift team was changing to go home. Sean, the duty doctor, was towelling his hair after his shower; she recognised his stocky build even though his face was hidden under a towel. And Marty, an intensive care paramedic like herself, was already dressed and was pulling his motorbike helmet from a locker.

'Morning, guys,' she said in greeting.

As Marty stepped away from his locker Georgie could see a third man at the end of the room. He was stripped to the waist, his jumpsuit top hanging on his hips. His back was tanned and smooth, muscular and strangely familiar. She could see two dimples at the base of his spine, just above his waistband, teasing her in a repeat performance. Georgie felt her heart rate increase. It couldn't be, could it?

He was turning around now at the sound of her voice and his abdominals rippled down his side. Did she dare move her gaze higher?

She lifted her eyes. Abdominals and then pectoral muscles came into view followed by full lips that were smiling, and above those a narrow, perfectly straight nose and grey eyes. Gunship grey.

Her eyes widened. Standing in front of her, semi-naked, was the cute doctor from yesterday. All that was missing were the Australian flag board shorts.

He was the new doctor?

She could feel her heart beating in her chest and she imagined everyone else could hear it too in the quiet of the room.

'You're Dr Wetherly?' She broke the silence but didn't apologise for bursting in on him while he was changing. Anyone who was at all self-conscious needed to learn to change in the bathrooms. Besides, she'd been treated to the same spectacular view yesterday and looking at this man's semi-naked body she couldn't think of a single reason why he might need to hide away. She swallowed hard, forcing herself to continue speaking. 'I'm Georgie Carides.' She took a deep breath and tried to relax.

'Please, my name's Josh,' he said as he extended his hand and stepped forward to meet her halfway. He was several inches taller than she was and as he closed the distance between them her gaze fell on his bare chest. Again. It took all her self-control to force her gaze up to his face. But even that was no great hardship. His grey eyes were watching her with amusement and she realised he was still holding his hand out, waiting to shake hers, while she stood there, staring at him. She couldn't believe he was the new doctor.

Quickly she clasped his hand, unprepared for the tingle that shot through her. It was the same reaction she'd experienced yesterday when he'd helped her to her feet on the pontoon. It felt as though he'd triggered a connection in her palm that led straight to her chest. Her breathing was shallow and rapid and her heart was racing. Again. Yesterday she'd put the feeling down to the adrenaline that had been flowing through her but that wasn't the case today. This time she knew it was all Dr Wetherly's doing. Josh.

'It's good to see you again,' he said. He appeared completely unflustered, calm and relaxed, behaving as though he was the old hand, while she felt completely disoriented. He let go of her hand and pulled a grey T-shirt over his head, before slipping his arms into the sleeves of his jumpsuit and zipping it closed. 'Small world.'

'Isn't it?' she replied, able to speak now that he'd let go of her and her breathing had returned to normal.

'You guys know each other?' Marty's voice came from behind her, startling her. She'd forgotten Marty and Sean were there.

'We met yesterday—' she told him.

'But I didn't know who she was.'

'You're in good hands, mate. Georgie's a good operator,' Sean said.

'We're going to be working together?' Josh's grey eyes hadn't left her face. He was watching her intently, almost as though he was committing her face to memory. But why he'd need to do that she had no idea. His gaze was intense and focussed but not obtrusive.

She nodded and remembered what had brought her in here. 'I'm the rostered paramedic today and our first call has just come in. A four-month-old girl in respiratory distress—she's in the Tully hospital but they're concerned her condition is deteriorating. Pat, our pilot, is just getting the flight details. We should be ready to take off in about ten.' That was better. If she concentrated on work, she could block out the image of a bare-chested doctor.

'The chopper's restocked and ready to go,' Marty said as he slammed his locker closed. 'Good luck, Josh.'

'Thanks, guys,' Josh replied as the night crew headed out the door. He turned back to Georgie, watching her with his grey eyes. 'So you drew the short straw.'

Georgie could see flashes of silver in Josh's eyes. The colour was striking. She forced herself to concentrate on speaking. Gazing into his eyes was not terribly professional. 'What do you mean?'

'You get to work with the new guy on his first day.'

'I don't mind,' she said with a grin. 'This way I can get you trained up just how I want.' And she didn't mind. She'd seen his CV and she knew he came with an excellent reputation, although she had expected someone older. Josh looked to be in his early thirties, pretty young for a specialist with his credentials, but that didn't bother her because this time she'd be in charge.

In an effort to stop ogling him, she opened her locker and threw her bag inside. She needed to get changed.

'I'll meet you outside,' Josh said as she slipped off her sandals and stowed them in her locker.

She turned to him and nodded. He was standing very close to her; she could have reached out a hand and touched him but she didn't.

As he stepped away she wondered if he was nervous about her disrobing in front of him? Surely not, she thought. He was a doctor, he'd have seen it all before. And he'd seen pretty much all of her just yesterday, she recalled. Her cheeks darkened a little as she remembered what she'd been wearing. Her black bikini hadn't seemed revealing out on the pontoon, not when everyone else had been dressed in a similar fashion, but now she felt her outfit yesterday may shown him more than she would have liked. She was glad of her olive complexion. Hopefully he hadn't noticed the blush staining her cheeks.

'See what other info you can get about the job,' she said

as she tried to quell her embarrassment. 'Louise should have a contact number for someone at Tully hospital.'

He nodded and said, 'No worries, I'll get onto it.'

He turned and left the change rooms, taking the image of Georgie Carides with him. Hearing her voice today and realising they were to be colleagues had been a surprise. A very pleasant surprise, he thought as he entered the corridor. Working with an attractive woman was always a bonus.

He could remember her features. Her face was round and almost perfectly symmetrical. Her dark hair was pulled back from her face and her widow's peak in the centre of her forehead further highlighted the roundness of her face. Her nose was small and straight and her olive skin smooth and tanned. Her almond-shaped eyes were the colour of chocolate and were accentuated by perfectly shaped black eyebrows. The only splash of colour on her face was the red of her lips.

Her natural demeanour seemed to be quite serious and solemn but when she smiled her whole face changed. Unsmiling, she was striking to look at but when she smiled she was beautiful. Her whole face came to life. Her teeth were brilliantly white against her skin tone and her mouth and eyes and eyebrows all lifted. It wasn't just her lips that smiled, it was everything.

He'd wanted to give her some privacy to get changed but it had been an effort to make himself leave the room. The room was unisex but it seemed wrong to stand around and chat to her while she was changing when they'd only just met. But when he recalled what she'd been wearing yesterday he'd been tempted to stay. He'd seen plenty of her in her black bikini and he could recall every detail.

Despite the fact they'd been working to stabilise a patient, he was able to recollect every one of her curves.

The curve of her waist as it had flared out to her hip. The curve of her bottom at the top of her thigh. The curve of her cleavage where the Lycra of her halter-neck top had pushed her breasts together.

He'd known he couldn't stand there talking to her while those images had been flashing through his mind, that wouldn't have been a very professional start to their working relationship. He had no plans to get involved with anyone during his six-month stint; but if there were more women like Georgie Carides in town, his time in Cairns was looking more promising.

Georgie swapped her singlet for a T-shirt with 'Paramedic' stencilled across the back and swapped her skirt for her jumpsuit, before pulling on socks and lacing her boots. Her hands were shaking as she tied her laces. She took a deep breath. Although she'd said she didn't mind working with the new recruit, she was nervous.

But it wasn't Josh that made her nervous. It was her reaction to Josh.

She knew plenty of cute guys but she'd never had the sense that they could affect her physically. She certainly hadn't expected to have such a strong reaction to him. Yesterday she'd put it down to adrenaline but today she knew it was more than that. She'd never experienced an instant, powerful physical attraction to a man and now it had happened twice in a matter of hours. It was unexpected and surprising, pleasant but scary—and it was making her nervous.

She wondered how she was going to be able to work with him. Would they work together smoothly? Would their styles be harmonious? Would she be able to concentrate? Questions buzzed through her mind as she zipped up her overalls. There was no way of knowing all the answers.

She'd have to rely on her skills and expertise. She was an experienced intensive care paramedic; Josh was an experienced emergency specialist. In theory she knew they should be fine. But in reality she was the one with experience in pre-hospital emergency medicine. She was the one who would need to take the lead, which meant she needed to be able to concentrate. Josh was used to working in a well-organised hospital environment and she knew, from her days as an emergency unit nurse, that hospitals were a long way from the chaotic, cramped, hot and dusty locations the emergency retrieval team often worked in. She needed to make sure she kept a cool, calm head. She couldn't afford to be distracted. A lapse in concentration could put her patients at risk. She couldn't afford to get sidetracked by cute doctors.

She closed her locker and headed out.

Josh was waiting. He held the door for her as they left the building and his stride matched hers as they crossed the tarmac and headed for the helicopter.

'Are you feeling okay? Ready for this?' she asked. She wondered if he was nervous, although he certainly didn't look it. He looked completely at ease. If anything, he looked calmer than she felt.

He nodded his head. 'Don't worry. I'm not a complete novice.'

He'd obviously guessed the reason for her question or knew what she was thinking. It would make her job easier if he had a vague idea of what he was in for. 'This isn't your first retrieval?' she queried.

'I've done a couple of transfers before but no primaries and no S&R.'

The most common retrieval for the QMERT team was

an inter-hospital transfer or IHT, which was what they were heading to now. Often, but not always, this was a fairly straightforward exercise and Georgie hoped that would be the case today.

Josh's prior experience of IHTs was a bonus and she was comforted knowing that his confident walk wasn't just window dressing, but, still, it was probably a good thing that their first callout wasn't for a search and rescue.

They were almost at the chopper now and she could see Pat in the pilot's seat, doing his pre-flight checks. Isaac, the air crew officer on duty, was stowing equipment. He closed the final hatch as they approached so it looked as though they were just about ready for take-off. She might just have time to introduce Josh to the rest of the crew but they'd have to check their equipment and run through their procedures in flight. She would have liked a little time to establish some rapport first before they were sent out on a job but, as often happened, the calls dictated their day and they'd just have to get on with it. She prayed it would go smoothly.

'Have you met Pat and Isaac?' she asked.

'Yep, first thing this morning,' he said as he raised a hand in greeting and Isaac nodded an acknowledgement.

'G'day, Georgie, Doc,' Pat greeted them, pointing backwards over his shoulder with his thumb, indicating they should board the chopper.

Georgie let Josh climb in first and she dragged the door shut behind them both, securing it with a flick of the lock. There were four forward-facing seats across the width of the chopper and another two rear-facing seats behind each of the flight deck seats. Josh had taken the third seat across. She could sit beside the door but she preferred one of the middle seats so she slipped into the seat beside him.

'Baptism by fire,' she commented as Josh strapped himself in.

She was relieved to see he was able to shrug into his harness, adjust the straps and snap it closed without difficulty. He seemed comfortable enough in the close confines of the chopper and she knew he'd flown before. Yesterday, in fact. She also knew he would have undergone the escape training course. All the rescue crews had to pass HUET—Helicopter Underwater Escape Training—because a lot of their flying could be over water. So transport wasn't a problem, but what she didn't know was how much medical experience he'd had outside a hospital situation. A few inter-hospital transfers wasn't much.

Pat had started the engine and the rotor blades were spinning. The noise made it impossible to continue a conversation until everyone was wearing headsets. She and Josh both grabbed sets and flicked the comms switch on so they could talk to each other and the air crew.

The chopper was lifting off its trolley. It tilted as it left the ground and the movement threw Georgie against Josh. There wasn't a lot of room to move and she could feel his thigh, firm and muscular, where it rested against hers. His body heat radiated through the fabric of their jumpsuits and into her thigh. She'd never experienced such a visceral reaction to someone before. It was as though her body recognised him despite the fact they were strangers. On some level she knew him. She could feel her knees trembling but she couldn't break the contact. There was nowhere to go.

There wasn't much room to move in the back of the chopper. She often felt as though she only just fitted in between all the medical gear and Josh was several inches taller than she was. He was really jammed in. She was five feet six inches. He'd be six feet at least. The stretcher was locked in place in front of them. It ran the width of the helicopter, from one door to the other, between their seats and those opposite. Josh's knees were crammed between the seat and the stretcher and now he had her practically lying on top of him as well. There was no escape for him, he was well and truly stuck.

'Sorry,' she said through the headset as Pat straightened the chopper and she was able to shift back into an upright position and away from Josh's firm thigh. Perhaps she should have taken a different seat. Squeezed up against him in the back of the chopper, she was a bit too aware of him.

'No worries.' He looked at her and grinned, apparently completely unfazed by the lack of room. Her stomach did a lazy somersault in response to his smile and the look of mischief in his grey eyes made her blush. Her body was overheating, from her thighs to her cheeks. She was stifling and she wondered if she could ask Isaac to turn the air-sconditioning up higher but everyone else looked comfortable enough. She'd just have to put up with feeling as though her cheeks were on fire.

'How did things go with Nigel yesterday?' Josh's voice was cool and relaxed, in sharp contrast to her flustered state. If he'd been surprised to find himself working with her he hadn't shown it, and if their close proximity in the back of the chopper rattled him he wasn't showing any outward signs of that either. Looking at him, one imagined that things were going exactly according to plan. 'Did he get back safely?'

She decided she needed to chill out. She nodded. 'No further dramas,' she said as she filled him in on the outcome of the English tourist's medical emergency from the previous day. 'He was admitted to the Cairns hospital overnight but when I checked on him this morning he'd had an uneventful night and they were expecting to discharge him.'

'The hospital doesn't mind you following up?'

Georgie shook her head. 'As you said, it's a small world.' She shrugged. 'Cairns isn't a big town, everyone seems to know everyone else and that's especially true in the medical field. I think the hospital staff expect us to ring. Most of the QMERT doctors work in the hospital too, and we all like to know what happened to our charges. Will you be doing any shifts at the hospital while you're here?'

He nodded. 'I'll do one or two a week but I'm in Cairns to get as much experience as I can with retrievals, particularly primaries. I imagine it's vastly different from working in a first-class A and E department.'

Georgie finally relaxed. This was her area of expertise and discussing this topic kept her mind focussed. 'You'll find you'll have to strip your medicine back to basics. The principles and the goals are the same, you just won't have the same state-of-the-art equipment at your fingertips or the specialist services you're probably used to. We become everyone from anaesthetist to scout nurse out here.'

'Luckily I like a challenge,' he said. 'So what should we expect when we get to Tully?'

For the remainder of the flight they ran through possible scenarios that might greet them on landing, including the possibility that they might need to intubate the baby. Together they checked the medical kits to make sure they had everything they might need. Small regional hospitals would have standard supplies but they might not always have the less commonly required equipment.

Josh was methodical in his checking but that wasn't surprising. It was a character trait attributable to most of the team—organised, meticulous and logical would describe almost all of them—and by the time they circled over the landing site in Tully Georgie was feeling confident that they would be able to work together comfortably.

She watched out of the window as Pat landed the chopper on the cricket oval. Tully had the highest annual rainfall in Queensland and light drizzle was falling as they climbed out of the helicopter and into the ambulance that was waiting to transport them to the hospital. Within minutes of landing they were walking into the tiny hospital.

The local doctor, who looked like he must only be just out of medical school, gave them a rundown on the patient's condition as they followed him to her bedside. 'Carrie is four months old but she was born eight weeks prem so her adjusted age is nine weeks. She's of Aboriginal descent and this is her third admission for breathing difficulties. The first two admissions we managed to control her and discharge her home with her mum. This time we can't get her oxygen sats up—they're actually falling.'

They were at her bedside now and Georgie and Josh both glanced quickly at the monitors showing Carrie's vital statistics. Her heart rate was 98 beats per minute, low for a baby, and her oxygenation was below 88 per cent. That was dangerously low. The medical staff had a tiny oxygen mask over Carrie's mouth and nose but the baby was listless and her chest was barely moving on inspiration. She was only just breathing.

'What were her oxygen sats when she came in?' Josh asked.

'Ninety two.' Even that was low, and if they hadn't been able to improve her saturation since she got to hospital Carrie was in trouble.

Josh checked the monitor again. Carrie's vital signs were unchanged. 'Right, we need to get some improvement in her vitals. We'll have to intubate to see if we can get her oxygen levels up and we'll have to take her with us back to Cairns. I'll need a straight blade laryngoscope, size one, and a 4.0 endotracheal tube,' Josh told her.

Georgie unzipped the medical kit she'd carried in with her. It included all the items they'd need for intubating an infant. As they'd had no way of knowing whether the hospital would have equipment that was small enough, it had been safest to bring it from the chopper. She passed Josh the items he'd requested and he deftly inserted the tube. Carrie was so sick she didn't resist and the moment Josh was happy with his positioning Georgie taped the tube in place and attached the ambubag. She would need to manually squeeze the air into Carrie's lungs and she'd need to do this all the way back to Cairns. But if it kept Carrie alive she was happy to do it.

As Georgie squeezed the air in they could see the baby's chest rise and fall with each pump. It looked like Josh's intubation had been millimetre perfect. She looked up from the infant and her gaze met his.

She was impressed with his skills—intubating a child of this age was no easy task. 'Nice work,' she said, and was rewarded with one of his heart-stopping smiles. He looked incredibly pleased with himself but not in an arrogant way. His grin was infectious and she had to smile back. Things were good. They'd succeeded. Carrie's oxygen sats and heart rate were climbing. She was stable enough to transport back to Cairns in the chopper. They would manage to keep her alive and get her to specialist care. Their first job together had gone smoothly.

By the time they were ensconced back at the Cairns base after transferring Carrie to the Cairns Hospital, Georgie had almost forgotten it was Josh's first day on the job. She'd ducked across to the Cairns airport terminal building to buy a drink and when she returned she could see Josh chatting to Louise in the comms centre. He was perched on the edge of the desk, one leg swinging lazily, looking quite at home.

Georgie walked slowly towards him, taking a moment to admire the view. His jumpsuit was undone and his grey T-shirt, the colour an identical match to his eyes, hugged his chest. She could imagine the ridge of his abdominals underneath that T-shirt. That image was burned into her memory from the day before. He was rolling a pen through his fingers and his biceps flexed with the movement, drawing her eye to his arms. She could remember how his arms had looked as he'd pulled himself through the water, the sunlight bouncing off his muscles as he'd swum out to the reef. He was an impressive sight.

She was within a few metres before he noticed her but when he looked up he greeted her with a smile. Even though Louise was sitting right beside him Georgie felt as though they were the only two in the building. How could he make her feel as though the rest of the world didn't exist with just one smile?

She was vaguely aware of the phone ringing as she smiled back at him. She forced herself to watch Louise answer the telephone, forced herself to concentrate on what was going on around her.

Louise was scribbling details onto a notepad. 'Male patient, early twenties, he's fallen from the back of a moving vehicle, severe head and chest injuries, possible spinal injuries. He's on a cattle station about a hundred kilometres south-west of here.'

Ten minutes later Georgie was back in the helicopter beside Josh. This time she'd deliberately chosen to leave an empty seat between them. She needed to concentrate. They needed to work out their priorities for when they reached their destination. The anticipated flight time was thirty to forty minutes and every one of those minutes would be spent making sure they had a plan of action so they could hit the ground running. A road ambulance was also on its way but travelling on dirt roads it would take closer to ninety minutes for it to reach the accident site. The QMERT team would be the first team on site. This would be Josh's first primary and Georgie needed to make sure they both had a handle on what they might be facing.

Through the headsets she could hear Pat checking the co-ordinates. They'd flown over the rainforest hinterland and the landscape below them was vast, flat and brown. From this height even the trees appeared two-dimensional, flattening into the dirt. Landmarks were few are far between. Thousands upon thousands of empty miles stretched into the distance, broken only by the occasional hill or river. Homesteads blended into the surroundings and were almost impossible to find unless the sun reflected off a shiny tin roof. They were searching for a couple of isolated vehicles on an unmarked dirt road. A task that was near impossible without the right co-ordinates. It was vital that they find the scene of the accident as quickly as possible. Every minute counted.

Pat had established radio contact with the station hands at the accident site and Georgie heard the radio come to life as a voice, crackly with static, filled their headsets.

'Is somebody there?' Despite the static, Georgie could hear the tremor of panic underneath the words. The station hand continued. 'He's not breathing. What do we do?'

'Can you feel a pulse?' Josh was calm under pressure and Georgie relaxed as her confidence in Josh's medical expertise grew. He hadn't put a foot wrong so far.

The reply came back. 'I think so,' said the station hand.

Georgie glanced at Josh. A more definite response would have been good.

'Can you get his mouth open?' Josh continued to give

instructions—keeping them busy would help to rein in any panic. 'Check that he hasn't vomited or that his tongue isn't blocking his airway. If he's vomited, you'll have to try to clear his mouth.'

'His mouth is clear but he's still not breathing.'

'Check his pulse again.'

'I can't feel it!' They could hear panic through the radio.

'You'll have to start CPR,' Josh said. 'Does someone know how to do that?' Despite the urgency of the situation his voice was still calm, his words and tone measured in an effort to decrease any further panic on the ground.

'Yes.'

Pat's voice came through the headsets. 'I can see the vehicles. We'll be on the ground in three minutes.'

'We're almost there,' Georgie emphasised. If they could hear them, if they knew help was close at hand, that would buoy them up. 'Can you hear the chopper?'

'Yes.'

Pat circled the accident. He needed to check the landing site before he guided the chopper down to the ground. As they circled Georgie could see two station hands kneeling in the middle of the dirt track as they performed CPR. Shredded rubber from a blown-out tyre was scattered along the road. The trailer attached to the back of the utility had jackknifed and was resting at an angle. A second utility and a quad bike were standing guard further along the road.

Josh slid the chopper door open the moment Pat gave them the all-clear. Georgie followed him out, running in a crouch to avoid the downdraught from the blades. She carried a medical bag in one hand and an oxygen cylinder in the other. Red dust billowed around them, kicked up by the spinning blades of the chopper. Georgie squinted as she ran in a vain attempt to keep the dust out of her eyes.

As they reached the scene of the accident the two station hands performing CPR stopped, obviously believing that since reinforcements had arrived they weren't required.

'Can you help him? Please, you have to help him,' said one.

'We had a tyre blow-out and Gus was thrown from the back of the ute. I think he landed on his head,' said the other.

'Keep going with the chest compressions while we do a quick assessment,' Josh instructed as he extracted a pair of thin surgical gloves from a pocket in his jumpsuit and pulled them on. 'You're doing fine. Keep going.'

Georgie also pulled on gloves, before kneeling in the red dirt beside Gus. He was lying on his back but there was a depression over his left temple and blood had seeped out of his ear. He must have landed on his head and hit the ground hard enough to fracture his skull. That was not a good start.

Josh was holding Gus's wrist, feeling for a pulse. He looked at Georgie and shook his head. Nothing. He quickly checked inside Gus's mouth, assessing the airway.

'I'll take over now,' he told the station hands, and they didn't argue about relinquishing their role.

Georgie worked with Josh, breathing through a face mask, breathing for Gus, but there was no change. During the flight they'd planned to establish an airway, make sure he had oxygen and get IV access. They hadn't planned on resuscitating him.

Josh continued with chest compressions. Georgie continued breathing. There was no change. He still had no pulse.

'I don't think chest compressions are going to be enough,' Georgie said. It had been more than three minutes and normal CPR procedure was getting them nowhere.

Josh nodded. 'I'll draw up adrenaline.'

On the assumption that doing something was better than nothing and knowing that chest compressions were more important than breathing, Georgie continued pumping Gus's chest while Josh searched through the medical kit. He drew up a syringe and felt for a space between the ribs before he pierced the left side of Gus's chest wall with the needle and depressed the plunger, injecting adrenaline directly into the heart muscle.

Georgie held her breath. Waiting. Her fingers on Gus's carotid artery.

There was a flutter of a pulse.

'We've got him.'

'Get some oxygen into him.'

Georgie started breathing air into Gus again while Josh pulled an endotracheal tube and laryngoscope from the kit. It looked as though they'd be doing another intubation.

Georgie did two breaths. She had Gus's head tipped back slightly and the fingers of her right hand were under his chin, resting over his carotid pulse. His pulse was barely evident. She stopped her breaths and shifted her fingers, searching for a stronger pulse. She couldn't find it.

'Josh, I've lost the pulse.'

CHAPTER THREE

'No, DAMN it.' Josh turned away from the kit and back to Gus, kneeling over him, checking for a pulse. He trusted Georgie's skill but he needed to double check for his own peace of mind. There was nothing. 'Resuming CPR,' he said as he began chest compressions again in a vain attempt to restart Gus's heart. If the adrenaline hadn't worked he knew it was unlikely anything else he did would have an effect, but he had to do something.

He worked hard for another minute. Another sixty compressions. There was no change.

He felt Georgie's hands over his.

'Josh, stop. His injuries are too massive. He's not going to make it.'

He didn't stop. He couldn't stop. He couldn't lose a patient today. He was in Cairns to get some pre-hospital experience but it was expected that he would be demonstrating his medical skills and performing well. Losing a patient on his first day was not part of his agenda.

He brushed Georgie's hands away and continued. Sixty-one, sixty-two. Another sixty and then sixty more.

'Josh, it's too late,' Georgie insisted. Her hands were back on top of his, stilling his movements. 'It's been too long.'

He listened then. He sat back on his heels, his hands

resting on Gus's chest, Georgie's hands covering his. He could feel her hands shaking. Or maybe it was his. He couldn't tell.

'We've done everything we can,' she told him.

He looked at her and he could see the bleakness of his own expression reflected in her chocolate-brown eyes. He could see she knew exactly how he felt.

'I know,' she said. 'We want to save them all but sometimes we can't. It's just the way it is.'

He rubbed his eyes and the latex of the gloves pulled across his eyelids. He stripped the gloves from his hands and tossed them onto the pile of discarded face masks and syringe wrappings, the detritus of the action. He breathed deeply. He could smell dust and heat and perspiration. He exhaled loudly and breathed in again and this time he could smell honey and cinnamon, an already familiar scent, and he knew it came from Georgie. Sweet and fresh, it competed with the smell of defeat.

The other station hands had moved back, giving Georgie and Josh some room. He looked up at them. They were gathered together, supporting each other. They knew the battle had been lost. He stood and went to them.

'I'm sorry. His injuries were too extensive. Even if you'd been closer to help, if we'd been able to get here faster, even then I doubt there's anything we could have done.' He knew his words would be of little consolation but he didn't want them blaming themselves or wondering if they could have done more. Today was just one day out of hundreds just like it. There would have been many times when someone had travelled in the back of the ute without incident but today Gus's luck had run out.

They stood in silence in the heat of the late afternoon. The bush was still, there was not a breath of wind and even the birds were quiet. Josh knew it was only the heat that was keeping the wild parrots mute but it felt like their silence was in deference to the situation.

In the distance he heard the sound of a vehicle approaching. First one. Then another.

An ambulance pulled up, followed by a police car, their distinctive markings almost obliterated by red dust.

Josh spoke to the policeman. He spoke to the paramedics. He was operating on autopilot. Gus was pronounced dead. His body would be put into the ambulance and transported to the morgue. There was nothing left for him to do here.

Pat and Isaac were helping Georgie load the equipment back into the chopper. He left the police and paramedics to finish up and went to help his team.

'Sorry, mate, tough day,' Pat said as Josh returned to the chopper. Josh appreciated his sentiment. Pat hadn't exaggerated the situation neither had he downplayed it, he'd said all that was necessary with those few words.

Josh climbed into the chopper and started securing the medical kits into position. The empty stretcher in front of his knees was a bleak reminder of what had happened. He unclipped one kit from a seat and strapped it onto the stretcher instead, partially covering the empty expanse. That was better. Less confronting.

The chopper lifted off the ground. As they banked to the east Josh could see the accident scene below them. The paramedics were closing the doors at the rear of the ambulance. The police were still speaking with the station hands. He closed his eyes, blocking out the tableau.

He should be saving lives in a big city hospital, with specialist help at hand and state-of-the-art equipment in place. He should be in control, not shooting adrenaline into a young man's heart on a dirt track out the back of beyond. What a bloody mess.

What the hell was he doing here?

He kept his eyes closed until he knew they were far away from the cattle station. Far away from the ambulance that held Gus's body. When he opened his eyes he kept his face turned to the window, his head turned away from Georgie. He didn't want to make eye contact. He didn't want to have a conversation. Not about what had transpired out in the red dirt. He knew he would have to think about it at some point. He'd have to fill in a medical report. A death certificate. But he didn't want to discuss it yet.

Georgie was quiet. Perhaps she was lost in her own thoughts. Whatever the reason, he was relieved she didn't seem to need to talk. Most women he knew would be attempting to have some sort of discussion, even if it was about nothing. The majority seemed to think that silence was there to be broken. He was pleased Georgie wasn't one of them.

The silence wasn't awkward. He knew she was there and knowing he wasn't alone was somehow comforting. He couldn't see her but he could feel her presence. He could smell her perfume, cinnamon and honey, warm and sweet.

He let the silence continue for the entire trip and it was after six in the evening and night had fallen before Pat started to guide the chopper down to the airport. In the distance Josh could see the lights of Cairns. They were almost home.

Cairns was a beautiful city by day and even more so by night, but it wasn't enough to lighten his mood. They were on their way home while Gus was on his way to the morgue. A young life extinguished. He felt the tension of the day in his shoulders. He sighed, a long, audible exhalation, trying to release the strain in his muscles.

He felt Georgie's hand on his. Her fingers entwined with

his in response to his sigh. Her hand connected him to the living. He knew her gesture was meant to give comfort and the warmth of her hand did exactly that. It warmed his entire body. He hadn't realised he was feeling cold but he was now aware of heat suffusing through him, bringing him out of his fog.

'Are you okay?' Georgie asked.

'I will be.'

'We did everything we could,' she said.

'Are you sure?' Today's events made him question his skills. He liked being in control of situations and, while he realised that was sometimes going to be difficult out in the middle of nowhere, what if things went wrong because of him? What if he didn't have what it took to work in this environment? 'It's our job to save lives. I'm no good to anyone if I can't do that.' What if he didn't have what it took to run an emergency department in a big city hospital?

'You said it yourself,' Georgie reminded him, 'Gus's injuries were too extensive. Even if we'd been able to reach him sooner, the outcome wouldn't have been any different. There was nothing else we could do.'

Losing a patient was never easy but Josh knew Georgie was right. He'd said those exact words to the other station hands. He and Georgie had done everything they could. But would others see it that way? He needed to prove himself. He needed to show he could handle working in this environment and losing a patient on day one wasn't an auspicious start.

He'd lost patients before, working in A and E it was inevitable, but today had felt very personal. He knew it was because it had been up to him and Georgie. A team of two when he was used to a team of three or four or ten or however many it took, and having greater numbers took the intimacy out of it. It didn't remove the responsibility but it did lessen the sense of failure.

As Pat guided the chopper down onto the landing trolley Georgie gave his fingers a gentle squeeze. 'Today was a bad day. They're not all like this. It'll be all right.'

He hoped like hell she was right.

Pat switched the engines off. The blades continued their revolutions but even the rhythmic thump-thump of the spinning blades didn't disguise the silence that enveloped the team within the chopper. Georgie unclipped her harness and Josh followed suit.

Georgie leant forwards between the pilots' seats. 'Dinner at my place when we're finished here?'

Josh heard her issue an invitation to Pat and Isaac. He was strangely disappointed not to be included yet there was no rule that said he should be. He was the new kid in town.

Their shift was over but it was their job to restock the supplies ready for the next crew and he knew following a routine would help to focus his thoughts. He got busy unloading the medical equipment they'd used and pretended he hadn't heard Georgie's words.

Georgie climbed out of the chopper and then turned and reached for the kitbags, preparing to carry them back to the QMERT building. 'The guys are coming back to my house for a feed. Would you like to join us?'

Yes, he thought. 'No,' he said, before thinking he'd better elaborate. 'Thanks, but you're not expecting an extra mouth to feed. I'll grab some dinner at the hotel.' He didn't like to feel as though he was imposing.

'Don't be silly. I wasn't expecting to feed Pat and Isaac either but we have a rule that we always have a meal or a drink together if we've had a bad day, kind of an unofficial debriefing session, and we certainly can't let you finish your very first day with us like this. There's nothing worse than going home alone with just your thoughts.'

'Are you sure?' After the day they'd had the prospect of his empty hotel room didn't appeal, neither did the idea of dinner for one in the hotel's restaurant.

'Positive.'

An evening in Georgie's company would be better than being alone in his hotel room. Looking at her now, even though she was wearing her QMERT overalls, which pretty well covered every square inch of her skin, he could picture her as she had been yesterday, in her black bikini, her olive skin darkly tanned, her petite figure perfectly proportioned. It seemed wrong, given the circumstances, to have that vision of her in his head, but he couldn't shake it. Perhaps he should take himself back to his hotel, he didn't need any distractions. But even as he had that thought he heard himself accepting her invitation. 'What can I bring?'

'Nothing. I've got a fridge full of food, I'm always feeding people.'

'She's not kidding, mate,' Isaac interrupted. 'Georgie's a great cook. Don't ever pass up one of her invitations.'

'I'm Greek,' she said with a shrug. 'It's what we do.' She smiled at him and her face lit up. It wasn't just her mouth that smiled, it was everything. Her smile had the power to make him forget about the day they'd had, just for a moment, and he knew that if he spent more time with her he'd eventually be able to forget the day for longer than a moment. And that had to be a good thing. He didn't want to forget about the boy they hadn't been able to save, but he did want something else to think about and he was more than happy for that to be Georgie.

'I'm going to have a quick shower here and then you can follow me to my place,' she said. 'Have you got a car?'

He nodded and twenty minutes later he was following

her little red car through the streets of Cairns and trying to block out the image in his head of Georgie in the shower. In his mind he could see the water running down between her breasts, her skin glistening wet, slippery and cool. Her long, dark hair was loose, slick and heavy hanging down between her shoulder blades, drawing his eye to the curve of her waist and buttocks. He told himself he was being ridiculous. He hadn't even seen her hair loose, it had been tied back both yesterday and today. He shook his head as he remonstrated silently with himself. He'd known her for barely twenty-four hours, he had to work with her, he had a job to do, he had no plans on starting a relationship. He pictured her in her black swimming costume instead. It was a little bit more demure, but not by much, but at least that picture enabled him to concentrate on navigating the streets.

He pulled into the driveway behind Georgie. Her house was a typical Queenslander. Constructed of weatherboard and raised off the ground, a section of the downstairs had been built in but the main rooms were upstairs. He followed her up the stairs and across the deck into the kitchen. She'd restrained her hair in a plait after her shower and it swung from side to side as she climbed the stairs, catching his eye and reinforcing the fact that her hair was tamed and not streaming down her back. His disappointment was almost palpable.

The house looked far too big for one person. When she'd said earlier that there was nothing worse than going home alone with your thoughts, he'd assumed she'd been speaking from experience. He'd assumed she was single. But perhaps he'd taken her words out of context, perhaps she'd been talking about him. Did she have someone waiting for her here? 'Are you sharing the house?' he asked.

She shook her head. 'No. I rented a large house because

I knew my family would all be visiting and would need somewhere to stay.'

'Visiting from where?'

'Melbourne. I'm from down south originally. I'm almost ten months into a twelve-month secondment to the Queensland Ambulance Service,' she said as she started pulling things out of the fridge. 'In the time I've been here three of my brothers and my parents have all visited. My last lot of visitors headed off to Port Douglas this morning. So you see, I can't share a house with anyone, it wouldn't be fair to subject them to my family.'

Hearing about the number of brothers she had distracted him from the realisation that Georgie wasn't from Queensland and she wasn't going to be here for much longer. 'Three of your brothers! How many have you got?'

'Only four.' She laughed and he knew she was laughing at him. The expression on his face was probably pretty funny. But he was happy to be laughed at, he thought as the sound resonated through him and lifted his spirits. 'I take it from your expression you don't have a big family?' she said as she passed him the salad ingredients, which he put on the counter.

'No, just one brother,' he replied. Who he didn't want to talk about. 'What can I do?' he asked, effectively changing the topic.

She passed him two beers. 'Can you open these for us? And there should be some onions in the pantry,' she said, waving her hand at a cupboard on the opposite side of the kitchen. 'You could chop them for me.' She pulled some meat from the fridge. 'I'll barbecue this. We can have yiros.'

Josh found a bag of onions and by the time he'd turned around from the cupboard Georgie had piled flatbreads next to the lamb and vegetables and had chopping boards, knives and beer glasses at the ready.

Josh twisted the tops of the beers and poured them into two cold, frosted glasses.

'Cheers,' he said as he handed one glass to Georgie.

He sipped his beer as he started chopping the onions. The cold lager quenched his thirst and he could feel the stress of the day ease slightly.

Georgie had slipped out to the deck to light the barbecue but when she returned he had more questions for her. 'What number are you in your family?'

'I'm the baby. And the only girl.'

'Does that make you a tomboy or a pampered princess?'

She picked up the tray of meat and looked at him with one eyebrow raised. 'I'm an intensive care paramedic, you tell me.'

'Tomboy, I guess.'

'You'd think so, wouldn't you? But I wasn't a very good tomboy. My brothers are a lot older than me and I was a bit...' she paused briefly, searching for the right word '...protected. Not pampered, mind, just discouraged from following in the boys' footsteps.'

'How much younger are you?' he asked as he traipsed to and from the kitchen to the deck carrying platters, crockery and food.

'Stephen is the closest in age to me, he's thirty-four so seven years older, the twins are ten years older than me and Tony's two years older than them.'

He couldn't imagine coming from such a large family but he supposed in many ways she'd been like an only child. Her youngest brother, Stephen, was the same age as him and he was keen to know more about her band of brothers, and about her, but the arrival of Pat and Isaac changed the direction of the conversation.

Pat opened more beers for everyone and proposed a toast. 'To Gus.'

They each raised their drink in respect.

'I hope some of his dreams came true. I hope he lived a good life,' Georgie said, touching her glass to Pat's before she turned back to the barbecue to baste the meat.

The aroma of garlic, onions and lamb teased Josh's sense of smell and his stomach rumbled. He moved closer to the barbecue, closer to Georgie, and leant on the railing of the deck.

'Did anyone find out anything more about him?' Josh asked. 'Did he have a wife? Kids?'

Georgie opened her mouth but hesitated before speaking and he saw her flick a glance in Isaac's direction. 'He got married about three months ago, one of the other station hands did tell me that, but I don't know anything further.'

'Poor devil,' Pat chimed in.

'I can't imagine what I would do if I lost Lani like that,' Isaac commented.

'Isaac is getting married in a few weeks and Pat is a jaded, cynical divorcé,' Georgie explained for his benefit.

'And what about you?' Josh asked Georgie. She'd said she lived alone but that didn't mean she didn't have a boyfriend somewhere. In Melbourne, if not here.

Pat laughed. 'It'd be a brave man to take Georgie on,' he said.

'Why is that?'

'She's got four older brothers, that's a lot of pressure for a potential partner to handle,' Pat explained.

'Why do you think I've run away from home?' Georgie asked as she scooped the cooked lamb off the barbecue and onto a platter. 'Isaac's fiancée is a nurse at the hospital.' She turned to Isaac as she placed the platter on the table.

'Josh is going to be doing some shifts there while he's in Cairns, you'll have to introduce him to Lani.'

Josh wondered at the very deliberate change in the direction of the conversation but he had no opportunity to question Georgie as she'd deftly shifted the focus onto him.

'You'll be working in A and E?' Isaac asked. When Josh nodded he continued. 'Lani's in ICU. Let me know when you're doing your first shift and I'll get her to introduce you to a few people.'

'Thanks, mate, I'd appreciate that.'

The conversation slowed as they all assembled and ate the yiros. Eating gave Josh a reason to stop talking, he didn't want to volunteer too much information. It was better to let them all think he was happy to be here and had joined their team at his own instigation. And by the end of the night he found he was actually enjoying their company. They were an easy group, welcoming and relaxed. Perhaps the next six months wouldn't be too onerous.

Especially not if he got to work with Georgie, he thought. His gaze fell on her again as she emerged from the kitchen, carrying yet another platter. Her plait fell over her shoulder as she bent forward to put the plate on the table and Josh had a wild urge to pull the elastic band from the end of her hair and loosen it. She straightened and flicked her plait back behind her shoulder and he had to be content with catching a whiff of her scent as she sat beside him. Cinnamon and honey.

'Who would like coffee and baklava?' she offered.

Baklava. That's exactly what she smelt like. But Josh knew the fragrance he could detect was Georgie and not dessert. He'd been aware of it all day.

Everybody requested dessert and Isaac had several pieces. 'Excellent, thanks, Georgie,' Isaac said as he popped another piece into his mouth.

'I've got a confession to make,' she said. 'My sister-in-law made this.'

'I don't care who made it, it's delicious,' Pat said, his mouth full of the sweet pastry.

Isaac finished another piece and drained his coffee as he stood up. 'Sorry, George, I've got to run. I'm off to collect Lani, she was doing a late shift.'

Pat followed suit. 'I'd better get going too. I'm flying you guys again tomorrow, I need to get a decent sleep.'

Josh stood too but after his initial hesitation to join them for dinner he was now reluctant for the evening to end. His lonely hotel room held even less appeal now than it had a few hours earlier.

'It's okay, Josh, stay and finish your coffee,' Georgie said as she put another piece of baklava on his plate. 'Eat that too 'cos the rest will get sent home with Pat.'

'You're a saint, Georgie,' Pat said as he kissed her cheek.

As Georgie wrapped up the remainder of the baklava and said goodnight to Pat and Isaac, Josh found himself wondering if Pat wasn't just a little bit enamoured with Georgie. If that was the case he then wondered how Georgie felt about Pat. Not that it was any of his business, he thought as he ate another piece of baklava. 'That dinner was delicious, compliments to you and your sister-in-law,' he said when Georgie returned to the table. 'Have you got as many sisters-in-law as you have brothers?'

'Nearly. Alek, one of the twins, isn't married yet.'

'Have all the sisters-in-law visited?'

Georgie shook her head. 'One to come.'

'So you've run away from home and almost all your family have followed.'

Georgie laughed and once again Josh found the sound of her laughter comforting. 'I didn't really run away. Not from my brothers anyway, they're harmless enough.'

He wondered what her reason for being here was. Something in her tone suggested there was more to the story than she was volunteering. What wasn't she telling him?

'So what are you doing here?' he asked.

'Same as you I guess, I came for the experience. In Victoria most people are within reach of a regular ambulance service so there's not nearly as much work for the helicopter team. It's mostly inter-hospital transfers and the occasional multiple-vehicle country accident. The distances in Queensland are so much bigger and the demand for the helicopter units is so much higher I can get twice as much experience in half the time up here,' she explained.

'So this is a career move for you? Work was the draw card?'

Georgie wondered how she should answer that question. The simple answer would be yes, but the honest answer was that she was escaping. Technically, she wasn't running away. She was planning on returning to Melbourne but she had needed to escape for a while. To escape from the life that was being mapped out for her. From her parents or, more correctly, from her parents' plans for her. All her life she'd played the part of dutiful daughter, baby sister or perfect girlfriend and she wanted, needed, a chance to find out who she was while she was on her own, away from the expectations of her family. 'Yes. It really is about maximising my experience in the shortest timeframe.' She went with an edited version of the truth. He didn't need to know more than that.

'And when you're not working? What do you do then?'

'When I'm not being a tour guide and chauffeur for my relatives, you mean?'

He nodded. 'What do you do in your spare time? You were out on the reef yesterday. Do you dive?'

'Was that really only yesterday?' Georgie shook her head in disbelief. It felt like days ago. 'That was me playing tour guide. My brother, Stephen, and his wife, were visiting. They are divers so I went out to spend the day with them. I was actually supposed to do an introductory dive but I chickened out. I had grand intentions of trying new things while I was here in Cairns but it turns out I'm not as adventurous as I thought.'

Josh laughed and his grey eyes flashed silver with amusement. 'Life is for living. You've got to experience it.'

'Believe me, as a paramedic I've seen what can go wrong when people try to experience things. I've decided I'd rather live to a ripe old age.'

'Come on, you must have done something slightly adventurous. You're a Victorian, you must have tried skiing, or have you done any travelling? Bungee-jumping in New Zealand perhaps?'

'I've been to Greece but that's about it,' Georgie said. 'Do you count being lowered from the helicopter by a winch as adventurous?'

'That's a good start.'

'A start! All right, tell me about your wild escapades.'

'What would you like to hear about, diving with Great White sharks in South Africa or heli-skiing in France?'

Georgie could feel herself growing pale just at the thought of those activities. Working as a paramedic, and prior to that as an emergency nurse, Georgie had seen the results of reckless behaviour too many times. There were some things she had no intention of attempting. 'You win. I'm not about to try to compete with that. Don't you realise life is precious?'

'Of course I do, I just don't think we should take it too seriously. We have to enjoy it. I went through a bit of a stage where I tried anything and everything with little regard for safety, but I've calmed down in my old age. Now I look for something middle of the road, somewhere between mundane and illegal but still fun. Could I tempt you to try something like that with me?'

Josh was grinning at her, his expression full of mischief, and Georgie could just imagine what trouble he'd got up to at times. All sorts of ideas flashed through her mind, most of which she wasn't about to share with him, but if he thought he could get her to agree to something dangerous just by smiling at her, he was mistaken. 'Like what?' she countered.

'Sky-diving?'

Not what she'd had in mind. She shook her head. 'No.' Definitely not.

'Scuba-diving?'

'Mmm, unlikely.' She'd hardly jumped at the chance to try diving yesterday. Josh might fancy his chances but she thought it was doubtful.

'White-water rafting?'

That sounded a little better. 'Maybe.'

'Excellent. A definite maybe!'

'That's a "maybe" maybe,' she said with a smile that morphed into a yawn.

'Okay, I'll work on your objections when I see you next but now it looks like it's time to call it a day.' He pushed his chair back from the table and stretched. His T-shirt rode up above the waistband of his jeans, exposing inches of toned abdominal muscles right before Georgie's eyes. She was tempted to reach out and touch him. She could remember how his thigh had felt when she'd fallen against him in the chopper earlier today, hard and warm and muscular, and she wanted to know if the rest of him felt the same. But while she was resisting reaching out to him he had lowered his arms and stepped away to push his chair under the table. 'Thank you for your invitation. You were right. I didn't want to spend the evening alone.'

She'd missed her opportunity. Not that she would have dared take it. Josh was a colleague and that meant he was out of bounds.

'And no one expected you to. I'm glad you came,' she said, remembering just in time to respond to his thanks as she stood and accompanied him down the stairs that led from the deck to the driveway.

'Can I repay your hospitality?' he asked. 'Can I take you out to dinner? I'd offer to cook but until I move into the apartment the hospital has organised for me I'm afraid the meal will have to come from someone else's kitchen.'

'I'd like that, thank you,' she said, meaning every word.

Josh pressed the button on his keyring and his car beeped as it unlocked. 'I'll see you tomorrow, then, and we'll make a date.' He opened the door but before he got in he leant down and kissed her cheek. His lips were soft and warm. She closed her eyes as his lips brushed her skin. 'Thanks again.'

It was just a thank-you kiss, she told herself as she watched him reverse out of her driveway. And his invitation to dinner was just a thank you as well. Josh was a colleague. And that was all he could be.

CHAPTER FOUR

JOSH was the first person she saw when she walked into the QMERT building the following morning. Through the viewing window in the wall of the comms room she could see him sitting at a desk, concentrating intently, not aware of her entrance at all. His head was tilted at an angle, he was propping his forehead in one hand, his elbow resting on the tabletop, and his biceps were bulging from the sleeve of his grey T-shirt. She could see the top of his head, his sandy blond hair sticking up in all directions; his face was obscured but she'd seen enough to know it was him. Seen enough to make her pulse race.

She wasn't used to this strange feeling of impatient excitement. She'd spent her life surrounded by men. Growing up, the house had been full of her brothers and their friends and now at work she was often the solitary female so she knew there was nothing special about men in general. She was used to all male company. They were just people. She'd never felt confused by them. Until now.

That was what was unfamiliar to her. Her reaction to him, the strong attraction she felt for someone she'd only known one day. Someone who, for all intents and purposes, was a perfect stranger. But he was someone who could set her skin on fire with one touch. Someone who could send her pulse soaring with one look. While there might be nothing special about most men, she wasn't sure if that description could be applied to Josh. Something about him was playing havoc with her senses. Something about him was constantly drawing her focus and she'd never felt so connected to someone she barely knew.

As she entered the comms room he dropped his pen onto the paperwork spread in front of him and rocked back on his chair. He ran both hands through his hair, a look of exasperation on his face.

'Good morning,' she said.

Georgie was pleased to see his look of frustration was replaced with a smile when he saw her. 'Hi. You have perfect timing,' he said as he retrieved his pen and pushed the papers across the desk towards her. 'Could you read through this and make sure I haven't missed anything?'

She glanced down at the paperwork. It was Josh's report regarding the cattle-station accident and Gus's death. That was what was bothering him. She wasn't surprised. Completing the form would mean reliving yesterday's events. It was a tough thing to do. 'How are you feeling?' she asked.

'I'll feel better once we get the autopsy results.'

'We did everything we could, Josh.'

'I know. I'd just like to have it confirmed by the pathologist's report.'

She sat at the desk and Josh moved his chair closer to hers, looking over her shoulder as she read through his words. He smelt clean and fresh, like peppermint, and she had to concentrate hard to make sense of the report. It was no easy task, reading with an audience, especially one who could distract her just with his scent. Eventually she finished. 'It looks right to me. Shall I witness it for you?'

'Thanks.' Josh passed her his pen and Georgie's heart

skipped a beat as his fingers brushed hers. Once again, just the briefest touch was enough to send a frisson of energy through her.

Get it together, she reprimanded herself. He's just a colleague. No different from anyone else. And she didn't want him to be any different. She didn't want to be attracted to someone. She wanted a break from all that.

But she had to concentrate hard to block him out as they were strapped side by side into the chopper, flying to Ingham for their first job of the day, a little later.

They were on their way to another inter-hospital transfer. The patient, Kevin, had come off second best when his motorbike had slammed into a tree on a wet road. He'd sustained multiple injuries, including spinal fractures and bilateral rib fractures, and his broken ribs had resulted in a flail chest and a haemothorax. He had chest drains in but he was critically injured and needed to be in a specialist unit. Ingham's small hospital wasn't equipped to manage his injuries.

Josh had completed his assessment of Kevin but as they started making preparations for the transfer, Georgie hesitated. Something didn't feel right and she knew neither of them needed another drama today. Not after yesterday's tragedy.

'Wait. I think we should intubate him before we move him to the chopper,' she said.

'Because?' Josh queried.

Because she couldn't cope with a second fatality on their shift in as many days. Because it was better to be safe than sorry.

'It's a two-hundred-kilometre flight back to Cairns,' she said. 'We'll be in the air for over an hour. If something goes wrong en route, we'll either need to land or try to intubate in mid-air. I don't know about you but I'd rather do that here.' In her opinion, intubating Kevin now would decrease the risk involved with the transfer and increase his chances of survival.

'Sounds reasonable.' Much to her relief, Josh didn't debate her suggestion. 'I'll give him a light anaesthetic so he doesn't resist the intubation.'

Once again, Josh made the sometimes difficult task of intubating a patient appear straightforward and Kevin was sedated, intubated and ready to transfer within a few minutes.

But ten minutes into the flight their treatment plan started to unravel. A high-pitched beeping rent the air. Something had set off the peak pressure alarm on the ventilator.

Georgie was closest to the machine. She checked the monitor. It was possible that Kevin wasn't getting enough oxygen. But the screen showed oxygenation at ninety five per cent, blood pressure 120/60. Both figures were falling but the machine looked to be working okay. It meant something was going wrong at Kevin's end.

'The ventilator's working—check the drain,' she said to Josh as she reset the alarm.

Josh was sitting opposite her and the chest drain was by his knee. He moved it. Nothing flowed out of it.

'It's either blocked or he's got a repeat haemothorax.'

The drain didn't appear blocked but a build-up of air or blood in Kevin's chest cavity could put pressure on the tube and prevent it from draining.

Josh removed a scalpel from the open medical kit beside him. The incision for the chest drain was visible on Kevin's chest wall above his arm. Josh enlarged the incision and inserted a finger to clear any obstruction in the chest cavity, but still nothing flowed through the drain.

The peak pressure alarm sounded again. The high-pitched noise was loud and intrusive, even against the background noise of the helicopter.

'Oxygen sats at ninety-four. His lips look blue,' Georgie reported. Kevin's condition was deteriorating before their eyes.

'I'll top up his anaesthetic,' Josh said. 'If he's starting to wake, he could be resisting the tube and that could set off the alarm.'

Georgie reset the alarm again while Josh topped up the anaesthetic.

'Pupils equal and reacting.' Georgie checked Kevin's eyes. She couldn't work out what was going on. Kevin was under anaesthetic and he hadn't lapsed into a coma, but his oxygen sats weren't improving and his lips were still blue. The drain wasn't flowing. Nothing was working. What had Josh said? 'Life is for living. You've got to experience it.' If they could save a life today, she was prepared to broaden her horizons and try a new experience. She was prepared to make a deal. 'If we get him through this, I'll go on one of your adrenaline-junkie escapades with you.' The words were out of her mouth before she could really think about what she was saying.

Josh finished injecting the anaesthetic into Kevin's IV and looked across at her with a raised eyebrow. For a moment she thought he was going to give her a chance to take back her impetuous offer but no such luck. 'You're on,' he said.

He looked at the monitor and then back down at Kevin. His concentration was unwavering. 'Right, what's going on with you, mate? I'm going to have to open him up some more.' Kevin's arm was lying alongside his chest. It hadn't prevented Josh from enlarging the incision slightly but he was going to need better access now if he needed to be more invasive. He moved Kevin's arm away from his body and with that slight movement blood began to gush through the drain. 'Would you look at that?'

Georgie could hear the relief in Josh's voice and saw him visibly relax into his seat as he checked the monitor. She followed his gaze. Kevin's blood pressure had quickly risen to 135/70 and his oxygenation was rising too. It looked like the crisis was over but she could still feel the adrenaline coursing through her veins. 'That was close.'

'We were not going to have a repeat of yesterday.' Josh replied. 'Not if I could help it.'

Georgie hoped Josh wasn't going to beat himself up over Gus's death yesterday. Thank goodness they'd managed to pull Kevin through. 'This is a tough gig, Josh. We're often working in difficult conditions with very little information. Things go wrong but luckily for Kevin things weren't worse.'

'Things came pretty close.'

'Yes,' Georgie admitted. 'But he'll make it, thanks to you.'

Josh still didn't look convinced.

Georgie frowned. 'Is something else the matter?'

Josh ran his hands through his hair as he let out a loud sigh. 'I'm not here for the experience alone,' he said. 'I do need exposure to pre-hospital medicine but I also need to show I have the necessary skills for this work. When I leave Cairns I'm hoping to return to Brisbane General as the head of emergency medicine but I was advised to have a stint up here first. I need to show I can work under this kind of pressure. I need to show I can save lives out of a hospital setting. I've already lost one patient and I don't intend to make a habit of it. I need to show I can do this.'

'Don't be too hard on yourself,' Georgie tried to reassure him. 'You've done an amazing job today. Kevin chose to ride a motorbike in wet and slippery conditions and you've saved his life. It's a good day.'

Josh was nodding. 'You're right. We won this round, didn't we?'

'We sure did,' she agreed. 'But being in this job and see-ing some of the odd decisions people make is why I don't like taking chances.' Now that the drama was over she'd forgotten about the deal she'd made.

'Oh, no. You're not getting out of it that easy.' Josh grinned at her and his grey eyes flashed silver with hu-mour. 'You have a choice to make. Sky-diving, scuba-diving or white-water rafting.'

Inadvertently she'd distracted Josh from his sombre thoughts but now she wondered why on earth she'd made such an impetuous call. 'There's no way I'm voluntarily jumping out of an aeroplane,' she said.

'Okay. On the water or under the water? What's your preference?'

It didn't look as though he was going to let her off the hook. 'Can we toss a coin?'

Josh patted the pockets of his jumpsuit. 'Don't seem to have one on me.' He grabbed an unopened syringe from the medical kit and hid it behind his back. 'Choose a hand,' he told her. 'If you get the syringe, you'll have to learn to scuba-dive.'

She took a deep breath and pointed. 'Left.'

Josh brought his hands to the front and opened both fists. The syringe was in his left palm. Georgie's heart plummeted. Seeing that syringe reinforced that she really didn't want to try diving.

'Can we try two out of three?' she pleaded.

Josh grinned at her. 'I guess that means you'd rather go rafting.'

She nodded. 'I guess so.' As much as she would like to

get out of the deal, she supposed going white-water rafting was a small price to pay in exchange for Kevin's life.
And if she got to spend the day with Josh, she wasn't really about to complain.

A few days passed without Josh mentioning white-water
rafting and Georgie allowed herself to hope for a reprieve.
Today it looked as though she was still in luck. Josh was
doing his first shift at the hospital, which meant he wasn't
at QMERT reminding her about rafting. But it also meant
she was working with Sean.

It was her first shift without Josh since he'd come to
Cairns and it was strange to be working with Sean again.
He was a funny guy with a dry sense of humour and
Georgie enjoyed working with him. He and his wife and
two young children had emigrated from the UK. He was
a good doctor but Georgie missed Josh. She told herself
it was because they'd developed a good working rapport
but she knew that was only half the truth. She and Sean
had a good rapport too, yet she hadn't missed him when
their shifts hadn't coincided.

She enjoyed Josh's company and the buzz she got from
being near him, and that element of excitement was missing today. Normally she would have thought her job was
exciting enough but since Josh had arrived that level had
increased. Even sitting in the lunchroom was more inter-
esting when Josh was there.

She was flicking through the local paper when Louise's
voice came through the intercom.

'Georgie, are you there? I've got Josh on the line for
you.'

She hurried across the room to pick up the phone. She
could feel her heart beating a little bit faster and as she
picked up the receiver she felt herself panting. She was

out of breath and feeling like she'd sprinted one hundred metres instead of just taking a few steps across the room. She breathed in deeply before she spoke. She didn't want to sound breathless.

'Hi, how's your day going?' she asked.

'Hi, yourself. It's okay, actually,' he replied. 'It hasn't been too busy. I had time to pop in and visit little Carrie to see how she's going.'

Georgie remembered the baby they'd brought back from Tully hospital on their first job together, and wondered if that was the reason for Josh's call. 'How is she?'

'She's doing well. She's had lots of tests done, there's nothing sinister, her chest is obviously just a weakness, most likely a result of her being a premmie, but her mum is expecting the all-clear from the specialist and she'll be taking her home soon.'

'That's good news. It sounds like you're finding your feet.'

'I'm doing okay, but I'm missing you guys. I feel like I'm missing out on the action.' For a brief moment Georgie thought he was feeling the same as her, off balance, but his voice sounded as though he was smiling and she could imagine his grey eyes sparkling as he spoke to her.

'You're not missing anything. It's quiet today and we're sitting around, twiddling our thumbs,' she replied. *And thinking about you.*

'I got the keys to my apartment today,' he told her. 'I've just been around there in my lunch break and although technically it's furnished there are a few things I'll need to get. What are you doing after work?'

'I probably should be going to the gym,' she replied. She tried to get to the gym three times a week; she needed to keep fit in order to cope with the physical demands of her job but at the end of a busy shift she often didn't have the energy. Today seemed like it was going to stay quiet so she should make an effort to exercise, but she wondered about the reason for Josh's call. 'Why?'

'What are you doing after the gym?' he asked. 'Would you come shopping with me? Point me in the right direction for the things I need. I'll buy you dinner afterwards.'

'I'd be happy to help you but I can't tonight.' She didn't have time to fit it all in. She had a previous commitment, one she wished she hadn't made, but it was too late to back out of it now.

'I'll take a rain check, then,' he said before he ended the call, leaving her wishing she hadn't agreed to tonight's blind date with a friend of her brother's.

'How did your date go?' Lou asked the minute Georgie stuck her head into the comms room at the QMERT base the next morning.

'Tedious,' Georgie replied. 'It was about as much fun as going to get my legs waxed. I've decided enough is enough. No more blind dates. No more dating at all. I'm staying single.'

'If you had a proper boyfriend, people would stop trying to set you up on blind dates,' said Louise.

'You stood me up to go out with a complete stranger?'

Georgie whirled around when she heard Josh's voice behind her. He stepped into the comms room and closed the door. He leant against Lou's desk and folded his arms across his broad chest. He was clearly waiting for her excuse.

'Sorry, it was a prior commitment, but if it makes you feel better it was a complete disaster,' she told him.

'You didn't tell me you had another option,' Lou reprimanded.

Georgie shrugged. 'Josh wanted me to help him shop for

his apartment but I'd already said yes to Costa. I couldn't cancel, my brother would have insisted I reschedule.'

'What has your brother got to do with it?'

'Costa has just been relocated to Cairns. He used to work with my brother Alek, and Alek thought I might like him.'

'Why are your brothers setting up dates for you? What's wrong with you?' Josh's grey eyes sparkled with silver lights as he grinned and baited her.

'Hey, watch it! There's nothing wrong with me!'

'There must be plenty of single men around if you want a boyfriend. What about Marty or Pat?' he continued.

'Don't you start!' she protested. 'Pat's forty! And Marty goes through women like a man possessed. Anyway, I'd have to be completely desperate before I dated a colleague. I've spent far too much time listening to them talk about women to ever want to put myself in the situation where I could be the one they discuss on a Monday morning.' She'd dated a colleague before and she'd hated it when everyone had known their business, sometimes before she'd known it herself. 'Besides, who said I even wanted a boyfriend? I'm perfectly happy on my own.'

'I just thought—'

She jumped in and cut him off. 'You thought you were helping but I don't need your help and I don't need a boyfriend. What I need is a project. Something to keep me so busy that I can tell my family I don't have time for dating. Actually...' She paused momentarily as a thought occurred to her. 'If you do want to help, you could be my project.'

'What?'

She nodded. 'I can tell my family I need to spend all my free time getting the new doctor up to speed. That might keep them off my back and it'll teach you not to meddle too.' She grinned and both she and Louise laughed at the shocked expression on Josh's face.

He held his hands up in surrender. 'I'm sorry, I didn't mean to give you a hard time. I promise to mind my own business from now on.'

'It's all right, I was just having a bit of fun.'

'Well, in that case, I'm sorry your date was terrible.'

'You don't look sorry,' Georgie argued.

'No?' He shrugged. 'I guess I'm not, seeing as it wasn't my fault. All I can say is you should have come shopping with me instead.' He laughed and Georgie was tempted to agree with him.

'I'll remember that next time,' she said.

'Here, I have something that might cheer you up,' he said. In his hand he held a stack of brochures and he passed them to her.

Every pamphlet had a picture of happy, smiling people wearing lifejackets. Happy, smiling people going white-water rafting. 'Where did these come from?' she asked.

'The tourist information counter in the main terminal building. Were you hoping I'd forget?'

'Yes,' she said. But she wasn't sure if that was true. She'd been planning on trying to avoid it but she had agreed to go. That was the deal.

She opened the top brochure. 'Which one looks good?'

'They're all pretty similar.' Josh took the rest of the pile from her and shuffled through it. He passed one brochure back to her. 'The girl at the tourist counter recommended this one. They've been around for a long time and have a good safety record. And it's on the Tully River, which has proper rapids.'

Georgie flicked through the brochure. 'What does that mean exactly?'

'It means you'll feel like you've done something challenging.'

Georgie pointed to the half-day option, 'So this one you think, "The River Challenge"?'

'No, that's for kids,' he said with a smile, almost daring her to argue. 'This is the one I think we should do.' He pointed to the full-day option.

'But that says "thrilling", not challenging.'

'I know. Sounds fun, doesn't it?' He was still grinning at her, his grey eyes flashing with amusement.

She raised one eyebrow in response as she read from the brochure. '"Level Three and Four rapids." That sounds okay if they're classed out of ten, not so fun if they're classed out of five. How are rapids rated?'

'Out of six.'

'Six!'

'It's okay. Only grade-six rapids have the warning "Danger to life or limb" so by the process of elimination that should mean that grades three and four are pretty safe.'

'Hmm.'

Josh wrapped his arm around her shoulders. 'I won't let anything happen to you, I promise.'

Georgie jumped when he touched her. She reacted as though she'd touched something hot when she hadn't expected to and that was how she felt, as though she'd been zapped by electricity. Why did he affect her like this? She needed to get away. She needed some distance, some perspective.

She stepped out of his embrace. 'We'd better go and get changed so we're ready if we get called out,' she said as she hurried to the change rooms.

But this wasn't one of her best ideas. In fact, it was downright idiotic. Because, of course, Josh followed her and the first things he did was open his locker and strip off his shirt. There was nowhere to hide in the unisex change rooms. Nowhere she could go to avoid Josh. And if she found it difficult to ignore her attraction to him when he was fully clothed, it was almost impossible to ignore it when he was standing beside her half-naked.

She put her bag in her locker, hiding behind the door to avoid ogling Josh's washboard abs. Not that it made any difference. She was perfectly capable of remembering what his body looked like: the image of him in his board shorts out on the reef was permanently imprinted on her brain.

'So are you doing anything on Saturday?' he asked. 'I know we're both rostered off.'

She pretended to be searching in her locker, looking for something. She found her hairbrush. That would do. 'Saturday? I don't have any plans.' She pulled her hairbrush out and turned away from Josh to look in the mirror and brush her ponytail but realised she could still see him in the reflection. He was pulling another T-shirt over his head.

'Excellent. Shall I ring the rafting company and book us on a trip this weekend?' he said as he tugged his shirt down to his waist.

Josh took his overalls from his locker and Georgie realised he was about to drop his shorts. Her breathing was suddenly shallow and she needed to look away. 'Okay. I guess I don't have an excuse not to do it. A deal is a deal.' At the moment she'd say anything just to get him out of the locker room so she could get her hormones under control. Her heart was beating like crazy and her mouth was dry. Her senses were fully charged. Why didn't she feel like that when she went on these blind dates?

She put her hairbrush away and plaited her ponytail, keeping her face hidden, using delay tactics until she was certain Josh had finished getting changed. Suddenly she wasn't sure how sensible this plan was, she'd be spending the day with Josh on the river and he'd be wearing next to nothing if the pictures on the brochure were anything to go by. She wasn't sure how she'd cope with that but it was too late to back out now.

'Come on, it'll be fun,' he said as he closed his locker. 'I'm sure I can be better company than your date last night.'

Once she heard his locker-door slam shut she dared to look again. He was dressed now and her breathing was under control again. She didn't doubt she'd enjoy Josh's company more than her blind date but she wasn't about to tell him that. It was bad enough that he seemed to know the direction of her thoughts. 'And if you're not?' She laughed.

'Then you get to choose the next adventure,' he said as he bent down to tie his bootlaces.

Once Josh left the change room Georgie collapsed onto the bench that ran in front of the lockers. She needed a moment to get her head together. She had to work out a way to cope with the feelings Josh evoked in her. She had to work out a way to get her responses under control when he was around.

CHAPTER FIVE

GEORGIE spent all the free time she had over the next few days cooking. Cooking normally helped her to clear her head but it wasn't having its usual calming effect this time. She alternated between trying to keep her mind off Josh and trying to work out why she was so affected by him so she could figure out how she was going to deal with it. But when he arrived to collect her for the drive to Tully she still hadn't come up with a solution.

He was wearing a grey polo shirt and camel shorts. He had good legs for shorts, muscular without being bulky. She glanced over at him where he sat in the driver's seat. His thighs where she could see them emerging from his shorts were tanned and covered with light, sandy blond hair. Strong and masculine.

She should have kept her eyes to herself because now she had to sit on her hands to stop herself from reaching out to touch him.

She concentrated hard to hold normal conversation as she tried to work out what it was about him that stirred her senses. She felt alive, alert and aroused. She realised he made her feel like a woman. It wasn't necessarily because of the way he treated her but more in the way she responded to him, to his masculinity. She was totally aware of him and, in response, she became aware of her own desires.

She'd have to accept that was how it was and deal with it. Ignore it. She certainly wouldn't act on it. She was taking a break from dating and she certainly wasn't about to date a colleague.

She managed to keep her hands to herself and her hormones in check until they reached the meeting point for the white-water rafting company. They left their car at the end point of their ride and were taken upriver by bus. At the launch site they were kitted out with lifejackets, aqua shoes and helmets. Josh took off his T-shirt and stood before her in his board shorts before he put the lifejacket on over his bare chest. Getting through that display without licking her lips was test number one. Test number two was when he helped her fasten the chin strap on her helmet and his fingers brushed against her throat, sending her heart rate soaring. She swallowed but managed not to hyperventilate. So far, so good. She hoped she'd get through the rest of the day as easily.

'I thought you said this was safe?' she said as she straightened her helmet and flicked her plait over her shoulder.

'It's just a precaution,' he replied. 'The company has an impeccable safety record. I checked.' He reached out to help straighten her helmet and her heart skipped a beat. 'You'll have fun, I promise.'

Georgie looked around at their group and suppressed a smile. The helmets they had to wear were most unflattering but she guessed she looked as bad as everyone else. The participants had been divided into four small groups and she and Josh followed their guide as he led them away for the safety briefing.

Their group, like the others, mainly consisted of young

backpackers, but fortunately most had enough command of the English language to be able to understand the instructions. Once they'd covered the basics regarding the commands, how and when to paddle or not to paddle and how to approach the rapids, they were allocated a position in the inflatable raft. Their guide, Darryl, sat in the rear, Josh was given the front position and Georgie found herself given a spot towards the back of the raft near Darryl. That wasn't quite where she wanted to be but she knew the raft need to be balanced and they couldn't choose their own positions.

Before they launched their raft Darryl instructed them to practise their war cry.

'Our what?' Georgie asked.

'Our war cry,' Darryl explained. 'Each raft has their own war cry. There are spots on the river where we compete to get to the next set of rapids and our war cry is part of the challenge,' he explained before he let loose with his catch cry. 'All for one…'

'And one for all,' his team responded.

From along the bank the other teams responded with their own cries and the bush reverberated with noise.

'You didn't warn me about this,' Georgie muttered to Josh.

He laughed. 'What's the matter? It's just a bit of fun. Just think of it as a team-building exercise.' Georgie's response was one raised eyebrow. 'You must have done things like this before?' he said. 'What about when you went to Greece, did you join any backpacker tours? Some companies are notorious for these types of stunts.'

'I went to Greece with my cousin and we stayed with relatives. I was barely allowed out of the house without a chaperone, so there's no way I would have been permitted to go off with a group of random twenty-somethings.'

She looked at the backpackers sitting all around her in the raft and thought how different her overseas experience was from theirs. But it was what it was.

'In that case, you'll just have to trust me,' Josh was saying. 'Let yourself go and yell, it's quite empowering.' To prove his point, he joined in with the rest of their group in a raucous 'And one for all' following Darryl's next command as they pushed off the bank and entered the water. Georgie had no option but to do as he said. The only way out of there was downriver and to reach the end they had to work together. She dug her paddle into the water, let go of her inhibitions and yelled with the best of them. Her reward was a big thumbs-up from Josh and a huge smile. The effort was worth it and made her determined to enjoy herself.

From her vantage point she could see Josh working hard, digging his paddle into the water, pulling strongly, his biceps flexing with the effort. He looked completely at ease. It was obviously something he'd done before and he seemed to relish the activity. She could imagine Josh alongside her brothers—they would enjoy rafting too. They were always on the go, always challenging each other to silly contests, always active. Josh was a lot like them, full of the joy of life.

She kept Josh in the corner of her vision as she concentrated on paddling and following Darryl's instructions. The section of the river they negotiated before lunch was relatively easy but they were still soaked when they stopped for a barbecue on the river bank. They dried out as they devoured the burgers but once they'd eaten Josh suggested taking another dip in the water.

'We've just eaten. What if I get cramp and drown?' Georgie protested.

'I'll save you.' Josh grinned as he reached for her hand

and pulled her to her feet. 'But if you don't trust me, put your life jacket back on and we'll just float about.'

Georgie picked up her jacket and slipped her arms into it. The river was wide and shallow in this spot and some rocks had formed a natural pool, cutting into the main channel. Georgie waded into the pool and floated on her back, drifting with the current.

Josh floated beside her. He turned his head and grinned at her, his grey eyes flashing silver. 'This is the life.'

She had to agree with him. This was perfect. There were no demands on her, there was nothing else she should be doing, and that was an unusual state of affairs. She was completely relaxed. And she had Josh to thank for that. She could be herself with him. He had no preconceptions about her. No knowledge of her as part of her large family. No knowledge of her as someone's daughter or sister or girlfriend. He was spending time with her because he'd chosen to and she was enjoying his company. But all too soon they were called from the water and directed to climb back into the raft for the post-lunch trip.

Georgie's confidence had increased and she was loving every minute of the experience. She laughed and yelled and occasionally screamed and she was still grinning and yelling encouragement as they approached the final rapid.

She couldn't believe how quickly the day had flown by. On the other side of this last rapid was the car park and kiosk that marked the end point of the day's excursion. One rapid remained to negotiate before the day was over. She couldn't believe how much fun she'd had. She'd expected to be totally out of her comfort zone, her sheltered upbringing and girls' school education hadn't prepared her for this. Perhaps she was really an adrenaline junkie. Perhaps, thanks to Josh, she'd discovered something about herself today.

They were neck and neck with one of the other rafts as they headed towards the final, narrow opening.

'Paddle hard, all for one,' Darryl yelled at them.

'And one for all,' they responded as they dug their oars into the water and tried to inch their nose in front of the other raft.

'Left side only,' was the next command, and those sitting on the right took their paddles out of the water, but their reaction time was slow and the other raft shot past them, taking first place into the final rapid.

As they emerged from the rapid in the wake of the first raft they could see the victors celebrating downstream. They had their paddles raised above their heads and were chanting their war cry. In the excitement of the celebration one boy stood up and his movement unbalanced the vessel. Because everyone had their hands and paddles in the air, no one was holding onto the ropes that ran around the inflated sides of the raft. As it tipped three rafters fell overboard into the river.

The raft righted itself as the weight distribution corrected and continued to drift down the river. Two heads emerged quickly from the water and those boys struck out for the raft where eager hands waited to pull them back on board.

The river wasn't particularly deep and the water here was relatively calm but the third boy hadn't reappeared. They all scanned the water, searching for him.

There. Georgie saw the red of the boy's lifejacket pop up behind a boulder. She pointed in his direction as she saw him trying to grab hold of the rock but the boulder was smooth and slippery with no purchase.

'I'm going in,' Georgie heard Josh yell to Darryl even as he was already slipping over the edge of the raft and into the river.

'What the—?'

Georgie heard the confusion in Darryl's tone. He was sitting near her, and she turned to explain to him. 'It's okay, he's a doctor—an emergency specialist.' She had every confidence in Josh's ability to get the situation under control. She'd seen him do it before. In fact, watching him swim away from her now gave her a sense of déjà vu. There was something immensely attractive about a man who didn't back away from a challenge, a man who was prepared to leap to the rescue and who had the skills to pull it off.

He'd reached the boy now. She could see Josh talking to him and, as Darryl and the other guide steered their rafts into the bank, Josh floated the boy on his back and pulled him to the shore but not out of the water.

'We've got trained first aiders, I'll get one from the office,' the guide from the other raft called out to them as Darryl gave orders for disembarkation from his raft.

Georgie was agitated as she waited for the others to climb ashore before her. As soon as she was able to, she hurried off to assist Josh, though she knew he was perfectly capable of managing on his own. There was no doubting his skill and medical expertise. She couldn't believe she'd joked about having to help him get up to speed with pre-hospital emergency medicine, he was totally in control of the situation, but she wanted to help. She wanted to be a part of it. It wasn't in her nature to be a spectator in these situations.

'Hi.' He didn't waste time with pleasantries. 'We need to get him out of the water but we'll need to be careful. I suspect he has fractured ribs and he's twisted his knee. There doesn't appear to be any spinal damage. His name is Ulrich.'

One of the rafting company's employees arrived with

a first-aid kit and a stretcher. Together Georgie and Josh rolled the boy onto the stretcher and with the help of the guides lifted him onto the bank.

Josh unclipped the boy's lifejacket. The jackets were cushioned at the front and back but along the sides, under the arms, the fabric was only thin. Georgie could see a large bruise already forming under the boy's left armpit. Ulrich grimaced in pain as Josh moved his arm but told them it was his chest that was sore.

Josh undid his own life jacket now that they were out of the water and slid it from his body. Georgie knew he'd want to get rid of its cumbersome bulk to give him freedom of movement.

He was bare-chested, his back tanned and smooth as he leant forward and extracted a stethoscope from the medical kit. He bent over the boy and placed the stethoscope on the boy's chest. 'Can you try to breathe in through your nose and out through your mouth for me?' he asked the boy. Ulrich did as he was asked but complained when he attempted a deep breath. He spoke perfect English but Georgie could detect an accent, possibly German, which fitted with his name.

'I know it hurts but try once more for me,' Josh instructed as he moved the bulb of the stethoscope.

'Equal air entry,' he said to Georgie. With fractured ribs she knew Josh would have been concerned about a pneumothorax but equal air sounds meant that was one thing the boy had escaped.

'He's not going to be going anywhere in a bus, you'll need to call an ambulance to take him to Tully hospital.' Josh was speaking to the rafting guide. He was issuing instructions, taking control of the situation, as Georgie had known he would, and everyone was running around doing his bidding, happy to have someone take responsibility.

Georgie helped Josh to sit the boy up so they could remove his wet lifejacket. She then carefully dried his upper body with a towel before covering him with a space blanket to keep him warm. Satisfied that the boy was able to breathe and hadn't sustained any serious chest trauma, Josh moved his attention to the boy's knee.

'It looks as though you've just twisted your knee. Nothing's broken,' he announced as he finished his examination. Darryl arrived at that moment with the news that the ambulance had been called but would take half an hour to reach them. The boy's friends trailed in Darryl's wake.

'Do you want anything for pain relief?' Josh asked Ulrich. A thirty-minute wait with fractured ribs would seem like a long time. When Ulrich nodded Josh searched the rafting company's medical kit. 'There's nothing really suitable, or strong enough, that won't interfere with the paramedics when they arrive,' he said to Georgie. 'In my car is a medical bag and there should be an analgesic inhaler in there. Do you think you could get my keys from our locker and find it?' Josh turned back to Ulrich. 'You don't have any medical conditions, do you? You're not diabetic?'

Ulrich shook his head and Georgie went to find their things and retrieve the car keys. She was familiar with these inhalers. They were carried in all the ambulances for short-term pain relief, and she found the box and slotted the cylinder into the bright green inhaler and returned to Josh.

Ulrich seemed much more comfortable once he'd self-administered the analgesic and the wait for the local paramedics became easier to bear. One of his friends travelled in the ambulance with him and Georgie and Josh stood side by side and watched as the ambulance made its way down the road towards Tully.

'I suppose that's the end of our foray into uncharted waters for you, then?' Josh asked her. 'You won't believe me next time I tell you something's safe.'

Georgie laughed. 'I'm pretty sure things wouldn't have gone haywire if Ulrich had kept his seat. He's only got himself to blame.'

'You haven't written me off altogether, then?'

'Not completely, but whether or not you get a second chance will depend on what you have in mind.'

'How about dinner? If we leave now we'll be back in Cairns in time for me to take you out somewhere.'

'Are you okay to drive all the way? You're not too tired?' It was a two-hour trip back to Cairns, a long way at the end of a busy day.

'Would you rather stay in Tully overnight?'

'No!' Georgie panicked. 'I was just going to offer to share the driving.'

The two of them, staying overnight in Tully. Together! Not that he'd actually suggested they spend the night together but she knew her resistance would be minimal at best if she found herself alone with Josh, away from home, overnight. Staying in Tully would only complicate matters. She needed to rein in her crazy fantasies.

'We're heading home, then?' he asked.

She nodded. Spending a couple of hours in a car with Josh would be enough to test her willpower and she thought even that might be a struggle. She couldn't be expected to stay away overnight with him and behave.

'All right,' Josh continued, 'let's head off so we can shower and you can choose somewhere for dinner. You will have dinner with me?'

Did she want to? She wasn't tired after the day of rafting. Adrenaline was still coursing through her system and if she was honest she'd admit she didn't want the day to end. Dinner would help to stretch out the day. 'Dinner would be lovely.'

Josh's grey eyes gleamed as he smiled at her and despite the streaks of dust and dirt on his face he looked fresh and alert, not in the least bit exhausted. Georgie wasn't sure where he got all his energy from but his smile was enough to give her a second wind and she looked forward to dinner with eager anticipation.

He took her hand as they walked to the car. His touch made her skin tingle. It felt alive, as though she could breathe through her pores. She felt as though she was floating and it was several moments before she even wondered about his easy, casual manner. She shouldn't be holding his hand but it felt so natural and so good she didn't want to let go.

On the drive back to Cairns Josh kept glancing at her even as he was driving and he would occasionally reach over to touch her arm or her knee as he talked. His touch was enough to keep the adrenaline coursing through her system and she was on the edge of her seat by the time they reached Cairns.

She hurried through her shower once he dropped her home. She was keen for their time together to continue. He was good company, he knew how to enjoy himself and he made her feel attractive, intelligent and amusing.

Which was exactly why she should keep her distance, she knew she should. She was supposed to be using this time in Cairns to find her independence, to find her own identity, and she couldn't do that if she was spending time with someone else.

So in an effort to attempt to keep Josh in the box marked 'colleague' she chose The Sandbar on the esplanade for dinner. It was a new restaurant and bar, not far from the hospital, and Josh's apartment, and it was super-trendy and busy so there was little danger of an intimate dinner for two. Georgie figured there was safety in numbers and she knew if she was going to be able to resist Josh she needed to avoid being alone with him. Every time she was alone all she wanted to do was touch him and taste him but she knew there was no point.

The bar was busy, as Georgie had hoped, but she hadn't counted on it being so busy that they wouldn't be able to get a table in the restaurant.

'If you don't have a reservation then I'm sorry but we're fully booked,' the hostess told her when she requested a table.

Josh intervened.

'If you could manage to swing it, I'd really appreciate it.' He focussed intently on the hostess and Georgie knew she'd be feeling like the only woman in the room. She knew that feeling all too well herself. Then Josh played his trump card. He smiled at her and Georgie saw the hostess cave in.

'I'll see what I can do. Come this way,' she said as she led them to a table on the very edge of a balcony overlooking the Cairns foreshore.

Josh held Georgie's chair for her as she sat. He ordered drinks for them and then proposed a toast.

'To new experiences.'

'Thank you for organising the rafting,' Georgie said as she joined in the toast. 'I really did enjoy it. I think maybe I am an adrenaline junkie in disguise.'

Josh laughed. 'Of course you are—you're a paramedic. I just can't believe it's taken you all this time to discover that side of you. What were your brothers doing when you were growing up? Why weren't you out with them, pushing boundaries?'

'I'm so much younger than them they didn't want me tagging along after them and my parents certainly didn't encourage it. I was, am, a good Greek daughter. I spent my time in the kitchen with my mum and Nonna. I wasn't out climbing trees and terrorising the neighbourhood with the boys. But after today I think I might be a little more adventurous.'

'Sky-diving?'

'Still unlikely.' She laughed. 'I know I told you I came to Cairns for the career experience but it was also my chance to try to discover who I am, away from the perceptions and expectations of my family, and today I learnt a bit about myself. I tested myself physically and I survived. I even enjoyed it, so thank you.'

'It was my pleasure.'

The waitress brought their order but as soon as they were alone again Josh continued the theme of the previous conversation. 'I'm intrigued. How do your family see you? Is their version very different to the one I see?'

Georgie shrugged. 'I'm the baby, the only girl with four big brothers. They all think I need looking after. That's why they're all looking for a partner for me, they see that as part of their responsibility, making sure I'm taken care of.'

'They're still searching for boyfriends for you? I thought you were going to tell them you're happy being single?'

'I haven't said anything yet. It's not that I mind the idea of marriage,' she explained. 'I'm just not ready for it. I need to work out who I am first. I just hope I can do that before my time here is up and I find myself back in Melbourne.'

'You're braver than I am. The idea of marriage frightens the life out of me.'

'Why?'

'Spending your life with one person, that takes a lot of commitment, a lot of trust. I think it's a lot to ask. A lot to expect.'

She smiled. 'Don't let Isaac hear your opinions. Their wedding is only a fortnight away.'

'I'm not against marriage for other people,' Josh clarified. 'It's just not for me.'

'Why not?'

'You're lucky to come from a stable, supportive family background. That immediately gives you a different perspective. Naturally you think the institution of marriage is a good one. Not everyone is as fortunate.'

Her family was immensely important to her and she couldn't imagine feeling differently, but it was clear that Josh didn't have the same rosy view of family life. She wanted to know more, she was desperate to know more, but something about Josh's tone stopped her from questioning him. Before she could think of another topic of conversation to break the awkward silence that had fallen, the waitress came to clear their plates.

The trade-off for securing a table for dinner was that they needed to vacate the restaurant by nine o'clock for another booking. Georgie still wasn't ready for the day to end; she didn't think she ever would be, but because she'd parked her car at Josh's apartment the day stretched further still. They walked along the esplanade together.

It was a beautiful North Queensland evening, warm and humid, but once the sun had set the humidity became pleasant rather than stifling. Josh took her hand as they crossed the street and instantly Georgie felt her temperature rise even further. His hand was warm and the heat, his heat, flooded her body. Their steps were unhurried but still she felt they reached her car all too soon.

Things had changed today. Despite her best intentions, her awareness of Josh had increased and her resistance was weakening. Every glance, every touch, every smile had gone straight to the heart of her, making her pulse race, her stomach flutter and her nerves spark. She wasn't sure exactly what had happened, she just knew that she wasn't ready for the day to be over. She wasn't ready to say goodbye.

She raised herself up on her toes and kissed his cheek. Her lips pressed against his skin, so close to his mouth that if he'd turned his head a few millimetres she would have kissed his lips.

'Would you like to come up for coffee?' His voice was soft and she could feel his words brush her cheek in little puffs of air.

She hesitated, running the different scenarios through her head, letting her imagination take flight before she replied. 'I really need to get home, I'm working tomorrow.' It had nothing to do with tomorrow, it was all about her lack of resistance to Josh. A coffee could mean so many different things. She'd learnt to take risks today but she didn't think she was ready for another one quite so soon.

'It was just a coffee.' He was smiling at her and his grey eyes were full of amusement.

'Stop doing that!'

'Doing what?' Now his eyes were a picture of innocence.

'Reading my thoughts.'

'Let me see if I read them correctly.' He leant towards her.

He was so close she could feel the heat radiating from him. Their faces were inches apart. He moved his head towards her, closing the gap.

Was he going to kiss her?

He stayed where he was for what seemed like for ever. How could he remain so still?

He was watching her, studying her, and then he moved another fraction closer, his head tilted slightly to one side.

Georgie shut her eyes as she waited for the caress she was sure was coming.

Josh's lips brushed over hers, the gentlest of touches, so soft she wondered if it was nothing more than her imagination. His mouth met hers again. His touch was firmer this time, more definite. Her lips parted involuntarily and she tasted him. He tasted of mint and she heard herself moan as his tongue explored her mouth. The outside world receded; it was condensed into this one spot, this one man.

CHAPTER SIX

HER heart raced in her chest and she could feel every beat as Josh's lips covered hers. She closed her eyes, succumbing to his touch. She opened her mouth and Josh caressed her tongue. She felt her nipples peak in response as he explored her mouth. His hand was on her bare arm and she could feel the heat of his fingers on her skin. She wanted his hand on her breast but she didn't dare move it there. She pressed herself against his chest instead as she kissed him back. Where was the harm in that?

Her skin was on fire as Josh ran his fingers up her arm. She melted against him. She was aware of nothing else except the sensation of being fully alive. She wanted for nothing except Josh.

She felt his hand move to her back. Her skin was bare between the straps of her sundress and her flesh burned under his touch. She felt her nipples harden further as all her senses came to life and a line of fire spread from her stomach to her groin. She deepened the kiss, wanting to lose herself in Josh, but a car horn tooting shattered the silence, interrupting the moment and making her jump. Her eyes flew open as Josh straightened up. Too late, she remembered where they were, standing beside her car in the middle of the street, behaving like a couple of hormone-fuelled teenagers. Her heart was racing in her chest and her breaths were shallow. She could hear herself panting.

Josh was studying her face as if committing each of her features to memory. His fingers trailed down the side of her cheek, sending a shiver of desire through her.

'Now would you like to come up to my apartment?'

She hesitated. The kiss was magical but it couldn't lead anywhere. Hadn't he made it clear at dinner he wasn't looking for commitment? It would be a one-night stand. That wasn't what she wanted.

She pulled back, breaking their connection. 'I can't.'

'Why not?'

'It's a bad idea.'

'It was just a kiss.'

Just a kiss! Maybe to him, but it had set her world on fire and she knew she couldn't be trusted if she followed him to his apartment. No, this was definitely a bad idea. 'You're a colleague. You're off limits.'

'Are you sure?'

She nodded. She couldn't speak.

'Okay. But let me know if you change your mind. No strings attached.'

No strings attached. It wasn't her style but it was tempting.

If he could play it cool, so could she. She smiled, striving for a casual tone, and said, 'I'll get back to you,' as she pushed the remote on her car keys and unlocked the door.

He bent his head and kissed her softly on her mouth, a brief brush of his lips, a gentle goodbye kiss, but her reaction was every bit as strong as when he'd kissed her more thoroughly. She used every ounce of willpower to make herself get into her car and drive away. But she watched him in her rearview mirror as he stood in the street and she knew she wouldn't be able to avoid him or pretend he didn't exist. She knew she couldn't pretend she wasn't attracted to him and she suspected he would become her forbidden apple, a temptation too strong to resist. One way or another she would need to get him out of her system.

Josh had got to work early and was chatting to Louise when they saw Georgie struggling through the door, carrying two large baking trays. She pushed the door open with her hip and nodded in their direction as she headed for the QMERT kitchen.

Louise watched her go before she turned to Josh and said, 'Something's bothering her.'

Josh wondered how on earth Louise had figured that out. Georgie had seemed perfectly okay to him. In fact, she'd seemed perfectly okay for the past few days, ever since he'd kissed her. He, on the other hand, had been completely rattled. Despite what he'd told Georgie, their kiss had rocked his world. It hadn't been 'just a kiss'. It had shocked him, surprised him, to his core. The moment he'd kissed her he'd had the sensation that he'd been waiting all his life to find her, all his life to have that kiss, and ever since then he'd been wondering how to persuade her to date him. What was the difference between him and any of the blind dates she was prepared to go on? The only difference he could see was that they already knew they had chemistry. But she refused to date a colleague and she'd refused to discuss it any further and he had no idea what he could do about that.

But why did Louise think something was wrong? What had he missed? What did Louise see that he didn't?

'How do you know something's wrong?' he asked.

'She's been cooking.'

Josh frowned. As far as he could tell, Georgie was always cooking. 'Don't forget we're all going to her place this weekend for Pat's birthday. Maybe she's run out of room in her fridge.' To his ears that sounded like a perfectly reasonable explanation.

'I'm telling you, something's bothering her. Go and find out what's wrong.' Lou glared at him and he half expected her to shove him out the door.

'Okay, okay, I'm going,' he said, fighting the urge to laugh. With a sharp salute in Lou's direction he followed Georgie into the kitchen.

Her back was to him as she slid the baking trays into the fridge. He dragged his eyes off her rounded backside as she stood up and turned around.

'Hi. Is everything okay?' he asked.

'I guess.'

Josh felt his heart drop to his stomach. She wasn't sounding like her normal chirpy self. Something was wrong. He wondered if he could fix it.

He crossed the room and put his hand on her arm, connecting them. 'What is it?'

'My parents arrive tomorrow.'

'I thought that would be good news.' In the time he'd known her she'd only had nice things to say about her parents and she seemed more than happy to have visitors.

She nodded. 'But they're meeting up with some friends here too.'

'And?'

'These friends have three sons.' She paused. 'Three single sons.'

'Let me guess, they're your next string of blind dates?' he smiled.

'It's not quite that bad. I don't think the boys are coming, but my parents think it's time for me to settle down and they're getting desperate. If it doesn't look like I'm going to find my own husband, I think they're not averse to helping me.'

'An arranged marriage?'

'That's not very twenty-first century,' she said, and finally he saw her smile. 'I don't think they'd call it that but they seem happy enough to send a few eligible bachelors my way. Or the bachelors' parents.'

'Why haven't you told them you're happy being single?'

'Because that's easier said than done. You haven't met my parents. That excuse would only work for so long and then they'd feel obliged to "help" me again.'

'Well, tell them you've already got a boyfriend.'

'Josh, they're coming to Cairns, they're coming to visit.' Georgie sighed. Hadn't he been listening? 'They'll expect to meet my fictitious boyfriend. What do I do about that?'

'Introduce me.'

'You? Why?'

He shrugged. 'You have a problem, that's one solution. I'll be your surrogate boyfriend. It'll give you your freedom back. Your parents can stop setting you up. It'll take the pressure off you.'

It wasn't a bad idea—in fact, she rather liked the sound of it—but she knew she liked the sound of it for all the wrong reasons. 'You don't want to do that. The experience could be a bit traumatic.'

'That doesn't matter,' he said. 'How long are your parents staying? A week? I can keep the charade going for that long.'

'Thanks for the offer but I wouldn't subject you to that.' She smiled and added, 'It's for your own protection.'

'What does that mean?'

'My last relationship ended because of my parents. Trust me, you do not want that level of expectation.'

'Didn't they approve?'

'No, quite the opposite. They loved Peter. So much that they wanted him to join our family. They started asking when we were going to settle down, offering to help us buy a house. Peter decided he wasn't ready for that commitment and headed for the hills. If you told my parents that's what happened, they'd be horrified. I don't think they're aware of what they did, but I don't want to subject each and every boyfriend to the same treatment. I don't want someone forced to marry me.'

'That's why I'm the answer to your problems. There'll be no forcing me to marry anyone! I'm offering my services and I guarantee I can handle parental pressure.'

She wished he was the answer to her problems but she doubted it was that easy. It was his fault she'd spent hours in the kitchen cooking, trying to clear her head. Her parents' expectations were nothing to cope with compared to her reaction to Josh. If she'd relived the kiss they'd shared once, she'd relived it a hundred times. She'd never spent so much time obsessing over a man, let alone one she barely knew, but she couldn't get that kiss out of her mind. She could remember how he'd tasted and felt and how the kiss had made her blood flow like molten gold and warmed her insides. For every second the kiss had lasted she'd spent as many hours thinking about what she should do, but when Josh walked into the kitchen she still hadn't made up her mind. Just the sight of him got her all flustered again. Her heartbeat kicked up a notch and her skin tingled when his fingers caressed her arm.

She shook her head. Her parents were definitely the least of her problems.

'They'd know something was up. They wouldn't be expecting you.'

'What does that mean?'

'You're not Greek.'

'You're kidding? You have to date Greek men?'

She shrugged. 'Pretty much.'

'Surely you've dated men who aren't Greek before?'

'Yes,' she admitted, 'but I've never seen the need to introduce them to my parents. It's never been anything serious and it would just make everyone uncomfortable. I don't need a pretend boyfriend. I don't even need a real one. I don't need to be rescued but I appreciate your offer.'

He shrugged. 'Okay, but let me know if you change your mind. I'm happy to help.'

'Thanks, but I'll manage. I'd better go and get changed.'

She appreciated his offer but it wasn't one she could imagine accepting. As if the kiss wasn't enough for her to ignore, now she had to ignore the image in her head of Josh as her boyfriend. The idea was delicious. He was delicious. But therein lay the danger. He was offering to be a fake boyfriend and she knew she might have trouble remembering that.

No. She was positive she could handle having her parents' friends here. Surely that would be easier than handling Josh. But knowing she had his support gave her some comfort.

Twenty-four hours later Josh was surprised to receive a frantic phone call from Georgie. Her parents had landed in Cairns that morning and he hadn't expected to hear from her at all today.

'Josh, it's me. Can you talk?'

'Why are you whispering?'

'I don't want my parents to hear. I have a favour to ask you. Remember when you offered to be my surrogate boyfriend?'

'Yes.'

'Does your offer still stand?'

'Why?'

'Mum has just told me that Con and Anastasia, the friends with the three sons, were making noises about bringing one of them up to Cairns to meet me. I kind of panicked, I'm definitely not ready to be set up by two sets of parents, so I took your advice. I told them I have a boyfriend and now they expect to meet him tomorrow at Pat's birthday barbecue!'

'And you want me to be your boyfriend?'

'Just for a week or so. Unless you've got any other ideas? Please?'

He had no intention of refusing, especially as it had been his idea in the first place. 'All right.' He was happy to do it, not least because he knew there would be some enjoyable perks to accompany the position of Georgie's boyfriend. 'I'll come over a bit early tomorrow and you can introduce me to your folks.'

'Thank you. You're a lifesaver. I owe you.'

Josh kept his word, arriving half an hour earlier than the other guests, and Georgie tried to get her heart to slow down and stop its frantic pounding. She was nervous and anxious. She hoped their plan wasn't a disaster.

He was carrying a large cardboard box, which he deposited on the kitchen table before kissing Georgie. His spontaneity startled her and she could feel her mother's eyes watching every move.

'Relax,' Josh whispered, and Georgie willed herself to stay calm. She knew Josh was keeping up appearances and she needed to do the same.

She introduced him to her parents, George and Sofia, and Josh pulled gifts out of the box, champagne for Georgie and flowers for Sofia, and then he set about helping with last-minute preparations, setting up the bar, putting out glasses, turning on the barbecue. He obviously remembered his way around the kitchen, he looked right at home, and his casual assistance lent authenticity to their charade.

When their QMERT friends began arriving, Georgie introduced them to her parents as Josh slipped into the role of host. As she watched Josh pouring drinks and handing around nibbles, Georgie realised she hadn't properly thought through their story.

What would happen if one of their colleagues alerted her parents to their fabrication? What would happen if her parents found out about their deception? What would their colleagues think? If she'd known she'd worry so much, she would have thought of a different plan.

She pulled Josh aside to ask him what they should do, only to find he'd already filled Louise in on their scheme and she'd told the others. Their secret was safe.

But the one thing she hadn't thought about was physical contact. Josh was very demonstrative and she realised she hadn't given this side of things any consideration. She didn't want to appear cool and aloof but she jumped every time he touched her. Which was often. Every brush of his fingers, every touch of his hand sent her pulse racing, and she grew more and more self-conscious.

Eventually, when she thought she was going to go crazy, she dragged him aside again and begged him to stop.

'Don't think you're overdoing it just a little?' she asked.

'Overdoing what?'

'The touching, the kissing, the looks.'

'The "looks"?'

He was laughing at her now. 'Stop it,' she said, trying to glare at him, but he'd made her smile. 'I think you've convinced my parents enough for one day.'

'Don't be a spoilsport, I'm enjoying myself.' He reached for her hand and hooked his fingers through hers. 'This is what people do when they're in a new relationship, when they can't get enough of each other. Before it all goes pear-shaped. Don't you remember a time when you couldn't keep your hands to yourself?' He brought her hand to his lips and kissed her fingers. Georgie had to clamp her lips together to stop herself from sighing out loud. 'I'm making sure we look authentic,' he said. 'I'm having fun.'

'I think you're having too much fun. Can you try keeping your hands to yourself? Please.'

'That's the first time I've had that request,' he said just before he leant forward and kissed her lips. It was just a quick kiss, timed to perfection so she couldn't resist or complain, and then he winked at her. 'I'll do my best.'

He walked away then and left her standing, rooted to the spot, looking after him as he did another round of the party, topping up people's drinks.

She took a deep breath. Her fingers were still warm from his touch and her lips were still tingling from his kiss. She needed to relax.

She went to find her glass. Perhaps another drink would help.

She finished her drink and tried to forget about Josh but she couldn't help wondering whether she'd made a mistake by asking him to do her this favour. She couldn't help wondering if it was all going to end in tears.

But the rest of the afternoon went smoothly. Her father was enjoying himself, mingling with the guests, but Sofia was spending most of her time in the kitchen. Georgie tried to get her to leave the dishes and go outside to enjoy the party, but she resisted.

'I'm happy in here and everyone pops in eventually either for more food or on the way to the bathroom. I'm fine,' she said as she started to assemble coffee cups and saucers on the kitchen table. 'So Josh is the one who took you white-water rafting?'

Georgie nodded in reply.

'I thought you weren't going to date co-workers after what happened with Peter,' Sofia said.

'Peter was a paramedic, Josh is a doctor.' It was all semantics but Georgie could hardly tell her mother it was irrelevant because it was only a charade. Fortunately Sofia had moved on to more important matters.

'His surname is Wetherly?' she asked. 'He's not Greek, then?'

Georgie suppressed a smile. 'No, Mum, he's not.'

'Well, your father seems to like him anyway.'

She looked across the deck to the barbecue, where Josh and her father were deep in conversation. She realised then it was too late to change her mind. Josh was doing her this favour and it was working. Her parents liked him and hopefully he'd buy her some time.

She wondered if she should rescue Josh but before she had a chance, guests began to say their farewells and she didn't get a moment alone with Josh until everyone had left, the dishes were done and her parents had gone to lie down.

Georgie made more coffee and took it out to the deck to Josh. 'Thank you for your help,' she said as she handed him a cup.

'My pleasure,' he replied. 'It went well. Pat enjoyed himself. It was a really nice thing to do for him.'

'He gets a bit lonely, I think. I wish he would find someone, I'm sure he'd like the companionship.'

'You're not planning on matchmaking, are you?'

Georgie shook her head. 'No. He says he's happy on his own and I'm the last person who'd interfere in that case. I hate that interference myself.' She sipped her coffee and asked the question she'd been dying to know the answer to. 'What were you talking about with my dad?'

'Your ex-boyfriend, Peter.'

'Peter! What about him?'

'Your dad was just saying that it was good to see you happy again after Peter broke your heart.'

'What? He didn't break my heart.'

Josh held his hands in the air. 'Don't shoot the messenger. They were your dad's words, not mine.'

'That's probably my fault,' she admitted.

'How so?'

'After Peter and I broke up I pretended to be more distraught than I actually was because it gave me a reason to escape Melbourne. I wanted to take the twelve-month posting up here but Dad would have argued against it—his single daughter moving to the other end of the country—but he gave in when I said it would help me to get over Peter. We worked together. He was—is—a paramedic too, and I over-emphasised the discomfort I felt at work after we broke up. But my move wasn't so much to do with Peter as it was to do with me. I wanted a chance to find my own identity, away from being a daughter, a sister or a girlfriend. This move was about a journey of self-discovery.'

'You can handle going back to your old job? Even though Peter is married?'

'He wasn't married when I went out with him. He got married three months later.'

'Sorry, that's not what I meant, but I thought he broke it off with you because he wasn't ready for a commitment?'

'That's what he said, but it turns out he just didn't want to commit to me.'

'And you're okay with that?'

'Yes, perfectly okay. Despite what my parents were hoping for, I didn't want to marry him either.'

'You weren't in love with him?

'No, and he didn't break my heart. I'm twenty-seven years old and still waiting to fall in love,' she said as she finished her coffee and took a piece of birthday cake from the plate in front of her. 'Have you ever been in love?'

'Yes,' he said.

Georgie was surprised at the wave of disappointment that flowed through her when she heard his answer. She wasn't sure what she'd expected him to say, he was thirty-four years old so it would be unrealistic to think he'd never been in love, but she hadn't realised she'd hoped he was in the same romantically barren situation as her.

'Was it a long time ago?'

He nodded.

'Was it the loveliest thing in the world?' She sighed. Despite being in no hurry to get married, she did want to experience her own very traditional, romanticised idea of being in love.

'Yes and no. I gave her my heart but it ended badly.'

'What happened?' She asked the question before she re-alised it might not be something Josh wanted to talk about.

'She was killed in a car accident.'

'Oh, Josh, I'm so sorry.'

Georgie felt mortified, as though she'd had the wind knocked out of her. She was so shocked she could barely talk. She sat in silence for a moment and then remembered he'd told her that that he didn't plan on marrying. 'Was she your soul mate? Is that why you said you won't marry?'

'No.' He was shaking his head. 'We were engaged but a few months before the wedding she came to me and said there was something she needed to tell me. It turned out she'd been having an affair. She told me because she was worried I'd find out anyway. I think if she thought she could keep it a secret she would have. We had a huge fight. That wasn't unusual, we had lots of ups and downs and usually I gave in, but not this day.' He paused slightly and Georgie wondered how long ago this had happened. It was obvious it still affected him deeply. 'I couldn't believe she'd behaved that way. I told her it was over, the engagement, us, everything. I told her I didn't want to see her again. I should never have let her get in the car but I didn't stop her and then she was dead. And it was my fault.'

'You weren't to know what would happen.'

'Maybe not but I should have stopped her. She was upset when she left, she was in no state to drive, but I was so angry I let her go.'

'When was this?'

'Eight years ago.'

'You're still blaming yourself?'

'No, eventually I realised that a lot of what had happened was beyond my control but it took me a long time to process it all and it made me think differently about relationships. I decided that I needed to be in control of my life and being in a relationship, to me, seemed to require giving up control. When my parents were still married there was a lot of arguing in our house, lots of yelling and screaming, lots of crying, lots of broken promises. I thought that was how families were. But to keep things together, someone always gives in. Tricia and I had a similar pattern but I was the one backing down. I didn't want to live like that again. I didn't want to be one of those people who spend their life fighting and arguing. I promised myself I wouldn't solve problems that way.'

'And have you changed?'

'I hope so but I don't really know. I avoid serious relationships, I don't want to put myself in that position again. I don't want to lose control. That's why I'm the perfect fake boyfriend—you know I won't fall in love with you and make things difficult.' He finished his coffee. 'But now it's time for me to go.' He stood and came around to her chair. He leant over her and kissed her softly on the lips. Georgie was surprised again, thinking this time it was a spontaneous gesture on Josh's part, but that was before he explained himself. 'Kiss me back, your mum is watching.'

He pulled her to her feet and tipped her face up to his. Georgie closed her eyes and waited for his lips to meet hers. His mouth brushed across hers very gently before he deepened the kiss. She tried to pretend she wasn't enjoying the experience but as his tongue teased her lips apart she sighed and opened her mouth and she knew she'd just given him part of her heart.

CHAPTER SEVEN

GEORGIE had seen Josh every day for the past week, at work or after work or both. He was playing the role of the perfect boyfriend perfectly. Her parents thought he was fantastic and Georgie had to keep reminding herself that he was acting. His acting skills were beginning to rival his medical skills.

She was dressing for Lani and Isaac's wedding but it was taking her twice as long as usual. Her hands shook as she zipped up her dress, as she applied her makeup, and they were still shaking as she tried to slide a silver clip into her hair to keep it out of her eyes.

Josh was coming to collect her to take her to the wedding and no matter how many times she told herself otherwise it felt like she was waiting to go on a real date. She was full of nervous anticipation and she was finding it hard to keep a clear head.

He had everyone convinced that he and Georgie were a serious item. If he hadn't told her about Tricia, even she might believe there was a chance he could feel something for her. But Georgie had the impression that Josh was quite content living his solitary life and was not planning on giving it up. But if she thought she had a chance to change his mind, would she take it?

Josh arrived just as she finally got the hairclip into place. Her breath caught in her throat when she saw him standing before her. He was wearing a light grey suit with a white shirt and he looked divine. The suit fitted his broad shoulders perfectly, the cut was exact, and Georgie guessed it had been tailor-made for him. The colour of the suit was a perfect match for his grey eyes.

'You look beautiful.' She thought he was reading her mind again before she realised he was complimenting her.

'Thank you,' she said as she smiled at him.

'You both look gorgeous,' Sofia gushed. 'Let me take a photo before you go.'

Georgie took her camera from her handbag and handed it to her mother. Josh wrapped his arm around her waist as she stood beside him and her stomach did a lazy somersault of desire. As she posed for the photo she reminded herself not to forget it was all make-believe. She was worried that the invisible line between friendship and something more was disappearing. She'd have to be careful to make sure she didn't blur the boundaries between their pretend relationship and their real one.

The wedding and reception were being held in one venue, the yacht club overlooking the Cairns marina, and there were plenty of guests already assembled when Georgie and Josh arrived. Isaac was mingling with the crowd, showing no sign of pre-wedding nerves as he waited for his bride, but Georgie only had eyes for Josh.

She'd felt a million dollars when she'd walked into the room on Josh's arm and that feeling stayed with her even when they became separated as they mixed and chatted with other guests while they waited for the ceremony to start. But even when he was on the opposite side of the room she had no difficulty finding him. It seemed she could find him through osmosis, almost as though she could channel his energy and feel where he was.

He was chatting to Marty but he must have felt her gaze. He looked across at her and winked and as the music started for the ceremony he made his way back to her side. The guests began taking their seats and with his hand resting lightly in the small of her back Josh guided her towards two empty chairs. As they sat he removed his hand from her back and held her hand instead. She thought she should tell him he didn't need to, her parents weren't there to see, but because he'd never listened to her before and because she was enjoying the contact she kept quiet.

Josh's attentiveness didn't waver throughout the evening. They were seated together at a table with their QMERT colleagues and even though they all knew the story behind their 'date' Josh continued to play his part. He held her chair for her, kept her water and champagne glasses filled and constantly touched her knee or arm to get her attention. Each touch of his hand made her blush and she was finding it difficult to concentrate on the conversation as his touch was so distracting. As Isaac led Lani onto the dance floor for the bridal waltz Georgie finally decided to let Josh off the hook.

'It's okay, Josh, everyone knows it's just pretend, you don't need to worry about me.'

'I don't mind,' he replied. 'It's easier to stay in character.' He leant back as he spoke and rested his arm across the back of her chair, brushing his forearm against her bare shoulder. 'I think it's becoming a habit.'

Georgie wasn't sure if she liked the sound of that but she didn't argue any further, content to sit and enjoy his company, and if he was happy to continue playing his role she wasn't going to stop him. But as other guests joined the bride and groom on the dance floor, Josh stood. He leaned over her shoulder and his voice was soft in her ear as he asked, 'Would you dance with me?'

She looked back at him and smiled. 'Of course.'

Josh pulled Georgie's chair out for her and smiled when she slipped her hand into his and let him lead her onto the dance floor. He'd been waiting for this moment all night. Waiting for an excuse to have her in his arms.

She was beautiful. He'd grown so accustomed to seeing her in her work overalls that seeing her in a formal dress was a revelation. It was as if he'd met her for the first time all over again. All evening he'd found himself distracted. Distracted by her and distracted by the sequins shimmering on her silver dress.

He took her in his arms and her cinnamon and honey scent wafted over him. He wondered if he'd just made a mistake. Would he be able to dance with her in his arms? He feared he might suddenly discover he had two left feet. But then she looked up at him, her dark eyes luminous, her lashes thick and long, and his feet began to move of their own accord as he lost himself in the depths of her eyes.

The band was playing a waltz and he pulled her in closer, letting the music wash over them. His right hand rested at the base of her spine, his left held her fingers. She fitted perfectly within his embrace. Her heels gave her enough extra height to make her the perfect dance partner for him and he guided her around the floor, his arm wrapped around her waist, her head just below his. Every time he breathed in he inhaled her perfume and he knew the scent of cinnamon and honey would always remind him of her.

Her dress clung to her curves. Its neckline was demure but the exposed skin on her arms was smooth and soft and delightful. Her hair was pulled back on one side and caught in a silver clip but it cascaded down her back in soft curls and all night he'd been longing to run his hands through it, to feel its weight in his palms. On the dance floor he could slide his hand under her hair and as far as he was concerned that was the next best thing.

He knew he was supposed to be playing a role but it was becoming more and more difficult to remember that. Her scent, her red-lipped smile and her soft velvet skin were becoming part of him and he had to fight to recall that their relationship was just a pretence. It was starting to feel real.

Georgie was getting under his skin. It was dangerous. He should be wary but he was positive he could keep things under control. He hadn't made a mistake so far. What was the harm in satisfying their desires? He'd promised not to fall in love; he hadn't promised not to try to seduce her.

He was sure the attraction wasn't one-sided but he had to make certain. He bent his head to hers, burying his face among the soft curls of her hair, and whispered, 'You look amazing.'

He was pleased to see he was able to make her blush. If he hadn't been so close to her he wouldn't have noticed the deepening colour of her cheeks. It was hard to see with her olive skin, but from a few inches away there was no disguising it.

'Thank you.' She smiled and her eyes sparkled and her teeth were bright against her dark red lips.

The song ended and the band began to play a more up-tempo tune. Josh couldn't keep Georgie in his arms but he wasn't ready to let her go. He led her onto the balcony overlooking the marina. It was his chance to get her alone, away from their colleagues. There was something he wanted to ask her.

'What are you doing after the wedding? Am I taking you home or would you come home with me?'

'Why?' She looked up at him and her eyes were twin pools of midnight, inky black and shining.

He knew this was dangerous. If she came home with him he would be mixing physical intimacy with emotional intimacy and that was something he didn't do. He should stop now, before it was too late. He should leave her alone, but as he looked at her in his arms he knew he wouldn't. He couldn't. He liked the way he felt when she was with him.

It had been a long time since he'd had a relationship that wasn't just about sex. It was dangerous but something about Georgie made him want to try it.

'Let me show you something.' He took her hand and pulled her close. The moment he touched her he could feel her soul. He could see her react to him. Her face was like an open book—every thought flashed across it and he knew his touch stirred her in the same way hers stirred him. He placed her hand over his heart. They were alone on the balcony but he wouldn't have cared if there was a room full of onlookers. Her hand was cool through his thin shirt. 'Can you feel my heart beating?' She nodded. 'Its rhythm is your rhythm. We have a spark. I want you to imagine how we could make each other feel. There is something real between us. It's not all make-believe. Don't ignore it. Don't fight it.'

'What do you want me to do?' Her voice was a whisper.

'Come home with me. Explore our connection, see where it takes us. Don't deny yourself that pleasure.' His heart throbbed with longing where it beat under the touch of her palm. He lifted her hand from his chest and kissed her fingers, slowly, deliberately, one by one, drawing out the moment of intimacy. Her eyelids fluttered closed and he knew she was thinking about his proposal. 'We can have a night to remember.'

He bent his head. He had one last chance to convince her. He put his fingers under her chin and gently tipped her head up. She didn't open her eyes and she didn't resist. His lips met hers. Her mouth was soft, warm, pliant. She moaned a little as he teased her lips apart. His tongue darted inside her mouth and she welcomed him, opening to him. He had one hand behind her back and he pulled her in closer, deepening the kiss. Her hands slid up his back and pressed through the thin fabric of his shirt. Her breasts were flattened against his chest. He could feel her nipples through her dress, hard and erect against his body, and he knew their attraction was mutual.

She was holding onto him as tightly as he was embracing her. Her hips pushed into his groin and he knew she must be able to feel his response to her touch. He let her kiss him back. Let her feel their connection.

'Come home with me,' he repeated.

'No.' She was shaking her head. Her soft, black curls bounced around her shoulders and cascaded down her back, distracting him. 'I'm not denying we have chemistry but I see no point in complicating things. This is make-believe. We are make-believe. Remember?' She gave a slight shrug that sent the sequins on her dress shimmering again.

'I remember. But it's only one night, it doesn't need to change anything. There's nothing to worry about. Nothing to be afraid of. No strings attached.'

Before he could beg, plead, argue or cajole any further, they were interrupted by the master of ceremonies. He was summoning everybody to the dance floor to say farewell to the bride and groom.

'I'm sorry, Josh, one-night stands aren't my thing.'

Georgie pulled her hand from his and moved away. It appeared the discussion was over.

He watched her go.

At least one of them had the sense to fight this attraction. He'd been mad to propose the idea.

He let her go. He couldn't have followed her even if he'd wanted to. He needed to wait for his desire to abate. It was several moments before he was able to leave the balcony, by which time the women had gathered around the edge of the dance floor ready for the traditional tossing of the wedding bouquet. He threaded his way through the throng to the peace and quiet of the far side of the room, away from the women, away from Georgie. But from the opposite side of the room he had a clear line of sight to where she stood. She was right in the centre of the crowd, surrounded by other women.

Lani turned her back to the female guests and lofted the bouquet over her head. The bouquet hit Georgie solidly in the chest. It was a natural reflex to catch it.

She could feel everyone's eyes on her but she could feel one pair in particular. Across the dance floor a pair of gunship-grey eyes watched her as she caught Lani's flowers. Over the delicate bouquet of frangipani flowers she met his gaze.

She stood still, holding the bouquet, as Josh turned and raised one eyebrow.

She wanted to go to him but she held her ground. She couldn't give in.

She had no doubt they would have had a night to remember and even though she could imagine in minute detail how the night would have proceeded, she couldn't do it. She was afraid she wouldn't be happy with just one night, and it could be nothing more.

He'd offered her sex with no strings attached but that was the trouble. She couldn't trust herself to handle that. It would be like playing with fire and she knew she'd be the one to get burnt.

They were too different. He was a confirmed bachelor, focussed solely on his career with no strong family ties and no plans to ever settle down. She wanted to fall in love, she wanted to be married one day, she wanted a family of her own. Their backgrounds, their views on life and love, they were all different. She wished for the chance to get him to open his heart but she didn't think she was up to the challenge. He wasn't going to change for her or anybody else.

She wished she could have gone home with him. She wished he was offering her more than one night but that wasn't going to happen.

He'd told her there was nothing to be afraid of. But he was wrong. She was afraid of getting her heart broken and in her mind that was plenty. He had promised not to fall in love. She'd made no such pledge.

She didn't think she could.

I could have danced all night and still have danced some more. Georgie couldn't remember the right words but it didn't matter, she knew exactly how Eliza Doolittle had felt.

She climbed the steps leading to her deck and twirled around, reliving the feeling of being in Josh's arms, of being swept around the dance floor. Since the moment the music had begun she'd imagined how it would feel to be in his embrace but her imagination hadn't been able to capture the delight; the sensation of floating on air, the warmth of his hand where it had rested in the small of her back, the firmness of his shoulder muscles under her fingers or the soft brush of his breath as his words had caressed her cheek.

She could have quite happily stayed in his arms until the sun came up. But she would have been a fool to take that option. A fool to open herself up to those feelings. She'd have to be content with the memories. And if that was all she was going to have, she was determined to hold onto them.

She held the bouquet of frangipani flowers in one hand as she opened the back door. She was still humming the tune as she walked into the kitchen.

'You sound as though you had a good night.' Sofia's voice greeted her as she closed the door.

'Mum! What are you doing up?'

'Your father can't sleep. I got up to make him a warm drink and now I'm wide awake so I thought I'd wait up for you. How was the wedding?'

'It was lovely.' Georgie sighed. 'Isaac and Lani were so happy and their mood was infectious. Lani looked gorgeous. I took more photos,' she said as she put the bouquet on the table and removed her camera from her evening bag. 'Would you like to see?' Georgie had planned to come home and take her memories of Josh to bed with her as some form of comfort but she couldn't ignore her mother.

They sat together at the table as Georgie scrolled through the photos. There were several of Lani and Isaac exchanging vows and several more pictures of the QMERT team, which Georgie had taken during dinner, and a couple of Isaac and Lani during the bridal waltz. Georgie thought they were the last photos but her mum continued to go forward and the next photo was one of her with Josh. She must have left her camera on the table when he'd asked her to dance and, unbeknown to her, someone had picked it up and snapped a picture.

She was wrapped in his arms as they danced. He was smiling down at her as she gazed up at him. To anyone who didn't know better, they looked like a couple in love. The camera had captured a moment in time when they had been unaware of anything or anyone else around them. They looked like they were in their own little world and Georgie realised that's how Josh made her feel. In his company she was content. She didn't want for anything else when he was with her. Thank goodness she hadn't gone back to his apartment tonight. Seeing the expression on her face in the photograph, she knew now she was in big trouble. She'd have to watch herself. She was falling under his spell.

'That's a lovely photo, I didn't realise it was quite so serious between you two.' Her mum employed her favourite tactic, make a comment sound like a question and see what information was forthcoming, but Georgie recognised the technique and kept quiet. She wasn't going to give her mother anything to speculate about; she'd learned long ago how to play that game. Besides, she didn't know what she could say.

After what seemed like a short lifetime her mum gave up. 'I'll just go and check on your dad. I'll be back in a minute.'

Georgie put her camera away while her mum was out of the room and took the opportunity to change the subject when she returned. 'Is he okay?'

'He's asleep. He hasn't been sleeping well recently so that's good.'

'Is something the matter?' Georgie frowned. She hadn't noticed anything.

'He's been very tired lately. He's blaming the lack of sleep but what I don't understand is why he isn't sleeping well. He's not worried about anything, he's relaxed, but he says he finds it hard to breathe.'

Now that her mother had mentioned it, Georgie remembered that her parents had been having afternoon rests, her dad especially, which was something he'd never done before, but Georgie had just assumed it was because he was on holiday and could lie down. Now she wondered what she'd been missing. 'Has he complained of shortness of breath at any other times? With activity? Have you noticed anything?'

Sofia shook her head.

'Has he been to the doctor?' Georgie asked.

'He's made an appointment for when we get home from this trip.' Sofia paused. 'Perhaps it's been bothering him more than he's let on,' she mused, 'especially if he's made a doctor's appointment. You know what he's like about going to the doctor.'

'Has he got any other symptoms?'

Sofia frowned. 'Like what?'

'Chest pain, dizziness, that sort of thing?' Georgie was worried. Her paramedic training made her assume the worst, even though she hadn't actually noticed any worrying signs herself.

'No. He reckons it's just old age. He's been talking about getting old a lot lately. I think that's why he's keen to see you settled down.'

And with those words Georgie had to rein in her fantasies once more. On her way home from the wedding she'd imagined what would have happened if she'd gone home with Josh. Now that she knew what it was like to be in his arms, what it was like to feel as though they were the only two people who existed, her imagination had been able to conjure up all sorts of fantasies.

She'd imagined the touch of his fingers on her knee as

they sat in the taxi, the warmth of his hand as he led her into his building, the heat that emanated from him as he pulled her against him in the lift, the taste of his lips when he closed his apartment door and kissed her, the breeze over her bare skin as he lifted her dress over her head, and finally the look in his eyes as he took her to his bed.

She could sleep with Josh to satisfy her curiosity and desire but nothing more would come of it. She remembered the photo of them dancing and she knew she wouldn't be able to sleep with him without exposing herself to heart-ache, she would be leaving herself wide open. She'd never had a one-night stand and she wasn't going to start now.

Maybe she should put a stop to this fake relationship before she got any more involved. Before it was too late.

CHAPTER EIGHT

GEORGIE was flat out for the next couple of days and it had nothing to do with work. She'd spent a pleasant day with her parents following Isaac's wedding, although she found herself watching her dad carefully, looking for any sign that he was unwell. Her parents were only in their mid-sixties and it was the first time she'd really thought about them getting old. Her dad was semi-retired; he was a builder and he'd worked hard and always been in good physical shape, but perhaps the years had taken their toll on him. It wouldn't be unusual. But Georgie had never imagined her life without her parents. Keeping a close eye on him while trying not to make him aware of her attention was difficult but thankfully she didn't see anything that concerned her.

Con and Anastasia arrived the next day and Georgie found herself playing tour guide to not one elderly couple but two. She'd organised to take them up to Kuranda, a town in the rainforest hinterland inland from Cairns. Travelling by a combination of cable car and old steam train, it was an extremely touristy thing to do but Con and Anastasia seemed to enjoy the outing and were appreciative of the effort Georgie had made.

But the combination of looking for anything untoward with her father's health and being a shining example of a perfect daughter meant she was exhausted by the end of the day and she was looking forward to returning to work.

Until she got there.

The first thing she saw on the noticeboard in the kitchen was photos of Isaac and Lani's wedding. That was fine, except that when she got closer to the board she saw that most of the photos were of her with Josh. Lou was in the kitchen, making herself a coffee, and Georgie knew she was watching her, waiting to see her reaction.

'Who put these up?' she asked.

Lou stirred milk into her coffee. 'Marty. He's taking bets on whether your relationship with Josh is happening for real now.'

'He's doing what?'

'He seems to think that you and Josh are dating seriously now.'

'And what about everyone else? What do they think?' She'd been off work for two days and this was what had happened? She couldn't believe what she was hearing.

'I think they'd be quite happy to believe it. You do make a good couple.'

'Not you as well, Lou?'

'Don't worry, I haven't put any money on you either way, I value my life too much.'

That was why this whole fake relationship was a dumb idea. She didn't want to be gossiped about. She'd conveniently forgotten all the reasons why she hadn't wanted to do this but Lou was rapidly reminding her. 'What about Josh? What has he said?'

'He said nothing's going on but it seems most people are choosing not to believe him.'

Georgie was mortified. 'Is he working today?' She had to find him.

Lou was nodding. 'He came in just before you. He should be in the change room.'

Georgie didn't bother saying goodbye to Lou, she bolted for the change room and hoped and prayed she'd find Josh alone. He was just coming out as she got there. She grabbed him by the arm. 'Can I talk to you? Somewhere private?'

'Sure. What's this about?' he asked as she dragged him outside. She took him around the QMERT building, on the opposite side to the helicopters—that way she was pretty sure they wouldn't be interrupted.

'Do you know what Marty's doing?'

'Running a book?' He nodded. 'Yeah, I know. Pretty funny, don't you think?'

'No, I don't think.'

He was frowning now. 'What's the matter?'

'This is just what I didn't want, people gossiping about me. This is why dating a colleague is a bad idea.'

'Fair enough, except we're not dating.'

'We know that but it seems everyone else thinks otherwise. All because I caught the stupid bouquet.'

Josh didn't think that was why people were talking. He'd seen the photos. He'd seen the way they'd looked when they'd been dancing together. Even in a photo their chemistry was obvious. It wasn't surprising that people were putting two and two together and he couldn't blame them for jumping to conclusions. He knew he and Georgie were acting the part convincingly, so much so that they were also in danger of believing the illusion.

'So what do you want to do about it?

'We should just cancel the whole thing. It was a dumb idea in the first place.'

'And what will you tell your folks?'

Georgie shrugged. 'I'll think of something.'

'No. We may as well keep going. How much longer are your parents in town for?'

'Three days.'

'And their friends are here too now, aren't they?'

Georgie nodded.

'I think we should stick with the plan. Everyone here will draw their own conclusions anyway. I don't think they'll believe we've called it off for a minute if they don't want to.'

'Are you sure you don't mind?'

'That people think we're getting down and dirty?' He grinned.

'No! Are you sure you don't mind being a surrogate boyfriend for a little bit longer?'

'It's fine. It's probably only a matter of one more dinner and everything will go back to normal.' Georgie's parents would leave and this would all come to an end then. But until then he needed to remind her, remind them both, that this wasn't real. Could never be real.

'If you like, I can tell Marty and the others exactly why I'm the perfect fake boyfriend. I can tell them why I'm never getting married, why I won't commit.'

'You're going to tell them about Tricia?'

He was positive he could make everyone believe it was all a show, Georgie included, but he needed to tell her his whole story.

'There's more to it than what I've told you. The others don't need to hear the whole story but I think you do.' It would ensure she wouldn't imagine their relationship to be anything other than the charade it had started out to be.

'My parents got divorced when I was a teenager. My dad worked for a big international corporation and he travelled a lot. Mum was bored, and lonely too, I suppose, and she had a few affairs. I think my father turned a blind eye the first few times and despite lots of fighting they managed to stay together, but I guess at one point he decided not to accept it and they split up. My brother and I were sent to boarding school. Dad was still travelling and I think Mum either didn't want the responsibility of looking after us or the reminder of what she'd done to the family so she chose a new life. Scott, my brother, was...' he paused and corrected himself '...is a couple of years older than me. He was the only constant in my life. I depended on him, trusted him, and that was pretty significant because trusting people wasn't something that came naturally to me. When I started dating I always expected my girlfriends to either leave me or betray me. I was always suspicious and that wasn't conducive to healthy relationships. I can't remember now whether I chose to trust Tricia or whether she convinced me but, in my mind, she was my first serious, committed relationship until she betrayed me. But her betrayal wasn't the worst of it. It was Scott's betrayal that almost destroyed me.'

'Scott's?'

Josh nodded. 'Tricia had been sleeping with Scott. That's what we were fighting about when she drove off, when she was killed.' He paused and took a deep breath. He never discussed the incident that had changed his life and made him into the man he was, the man who couldn't commit, but Georgie needed to hear this. She needed to understand him.

'She'd been having an affair with your brother?' Georgie's dark eyes were wide with surprise. 'How could they do that to you?'

'I don't know. I couldn't understand it and I certainly couldn't accept it. Scott and I were always very competitive, as I think most brothers are, but I never expected him to steal my fiancée. He was my big brother. I thought he'd look out for me. I thought we'd look out for each other, but I was wrong. I went a little bit crazy after that. I took time off university, went travelling, looking for the most dangerous activities and situations I could find, the more outrageous the better. I was feeling sorry for myself, testing my own mortality, trying to decide if life was worth living.'

'And you decided it was?'

'Yes, but I promised myself I'd never put myself in a situation like that again, so I concentrated on work and avoided my brother and relationships in general.'

'Do you see your brother now?'

He shook his head. 'No. My experience of relationships has all been about arguing, fighting and betrayal. That's why I don't plan on getting married. I have nothing left in me to give anyone. If I can't trust, what's the point? But I can tell everyone about Tricia. That'll give them something else to gossip about instead.'

'No.' Georgie shook her head. Three days, that's all it was. She could manage three more days. 'You don't need to tell them about Tricia. I'd rather let everyone jump to conclusions for a few more days than make you divulge your secrets.' Marty could take bets but she wouldn't give him any more fodder for gossip. 'My parents will be gone soon and this will all be over. If you can manage one more dinner, that'll keep my parents happy and then things will be back to normal.'

Only two more days now, she thought the next morning as she parked her car outside the QMERT building, but even so she found herself automatically searching for Josh's car as she locked hers. Just thinking about seeing him again made her heart race.

Georgie disagreed about his assessment that he had

nothing to give but she knew it wasn't her place to say so. He was doing her a favour; he hadn't asked her to interfere in his life. In two days there would be no need to have any extra contact with Josh.

She'd let herself get carried away with their charade but hearing Josh's story had reminded her of the truth. She suspected that's why he'd told her and she knew she had to keep her feelings under control. She had to remember their relationship wasn't going anywhere. Had to remember they didn't actually have a relationship and they definitely didn't have a future.

She waited for her heart rate to return to normal, waited until she was sure she could behave normally around Josh, before she gathered her things and went into work, only to find he was doing a shift at the hospital. But at least with him out of the way she knew she'd be able to keep her mind on her job.

But he wasn't completely out of contact. The crew was on their second run of the day, a routine inter-hospital transfer, when Louise patched a phone call through to the chopper.

'Georgie, I have an urgent phone call for you. It's Josh.'

Louise's message immediately sent her into a spin. She wondered what Josh could possibly want that would require him to go to the trouble of tracking her down in the chopper.

'Josh, what's up?'

'Where are you guys?'

His tone was short, abrupt even. His phone manner left a lot to be desired but as the call was coming through the helicopter radio she gave him the benefit of the doubt. Maybe it was because he knew everyone in the chopper could hear the conversation through their headsets.

'We're heading to Dimbulah,' she told him.

'You're on your way there now?'

'Yes, we're about twenty minutes east of town.'

'I have something I need to tell you.' He paused very slightly and Georgie frowned. There was complete silence through the radio and it felt as though minutes had passed before she heard his next words. 'Everyone is okay but your father has just been brought into Emergency with chest pain.'

Immediately Georgie recalled her father's shortness of breath. 'Is he having a heart attack?' Why hadn't she insisted that he have a check-up with a doctor while he was in Cairns? Why had she been content for him to wait until he got home to Melbourne? Even though she'd seen no sign of any problems she still berated herself. Her mother had told her of the episodes—why had she ignored her?

'We're running tests now,' he said.

'It'll be a few hours before I'm back in Cairns. How serious is this?' She could hear the panic in her voice. Was there more that Josh wasn't telling her?

'It's okay, Georgie, you can relax. We've got things under control.' Hearing him say her name calmed her nerves. He sounded so assured and confident. He'd tell her straight, wouldn't he? 'If I thought it was critical I'd tell you,' he continued. Even over the radio it seemed as though he could follow her thoughts. 'The ECG isn't showing any signs of cardiac arrhythmia but we'll keep testing until we find out what's going on. I'll take care of him but come in when you get back.'

She breathed out, concentrating on expelling the air, releasing the tension. If Josh said he'd take care of things she trusted him to do just that. 'Have you seen Mum? Is she okay?'

'She seems to be. She's with Con and Anastasia.' He knew who they were and now he'd met them, but it was still strange to hear him mention her parents' friends. It was as though they had no secrets, as though he knew all the intimate details of her life, but fortunately he didn't disclose anything further. He hadn't forgotten that the rest of the crew could hear their entire conversation. 'Don't worry, everything will be all right. I'll keep you up to date. See you when you get back.'

'Thanks, Josh.'

She worked hard to keep her focus and concentration on the job and fortunately the IHT was straightforward and the return to Cairns went smoothly. Josh phoned with another update as they were returning to Cairns. Her father's condition had stabilised and he'd been transferred to one of the cardiology beds, and this news helped to settle her nerves.

It was nearing the end of her shift when the chopper landed opposite the hospital to transfer their patient. Sean suggested that Georgie stay behind and she gratefully accepted.

'Pat and I will get your car back to you somehow,' he said. 'And Louise can call Marty and see if he can come in a bit early in case we need a paramedic. Don't worry about us, go and see your dad.'

She didn't need to be asked twice. She and Sean transferred their patient to the hospital but Georgie didn't return to the chopper, heading instead for the cardiology ward. Her mum was in a chair beside her father but Georgie was pleased to see there were no other visitors. Con and Anastasia must have returned to their hotel.

'Dad! How are you feeling?' she asked as she kissed both her parents.

'Completely fine,' George said. 'If I wasn't hooked up to these monitors I'd walk out of here. It was just a bit of indigestion, I'm sure of it.'

'You don't have any pain? Any discomfort?'

'None. I feel like a fraud.'

Georgie's gaze flicked to the monitor. According to the figures George was okay. His oxygen sats, blood pressure and heart rate were all within normal limits. But that didn't explain why he'd been admitted.

'Tell me what happened this morning.'

'Your mother and I had breakfast with Con and Anastasia and then we went for a walk along the esplanade so they could have a look around Cairns. I had a bit of chest pain, which I'm sure was indigestion—'

'There was a bit more to it than that, George,' Sofia interrupted her husband. 'You felt a bit dizzy too.'

'I'm not used to the heat, that's all,' George insisted. 'I didn't have any arm pain or anything else.'

Sofia ignored him and turned to her daughter. 'We were right by the hospital so, in view of his other recent complaints about shortness of breath, I thought he should get checked out.'

'That was the right thing to do,' Georgie responded. With chest pain, dizziness and a history of shortness of breath, it was no surprise her father had been admitted to the cardiology ward. There was definitely something abnormal going on. 'What have the doctors told you? What have they found?'

'I think they said the major arteries are okay but they're going to do more tests tomorrow.'

Movement in the doorway distracted George, and Georgie turned to see what, or who, her father was looking at.

It was Josh.

'Hello, you're here,' he said as he entered the room, and with those few words he managed to make it sound as though he'd been counting the minutes until she arrived. He made it sound as though he'd missed her.

His eyes locked with hers and he smiled. His grey eyes sparkled silver and his smile said he was there for her. His dark blond hair was sticking up and he had a slight shadow of beard darkening his jaw. He looked good. She smiled in return and took a step towards him before she hesitated. She wasn't sure how she should be behaving. But Josh didn't hesitate. He stepped forward and took her in his arms.

'What are you doing?' she whispered.

He leant down and his lips pressed against her hair. 'I'm comforting you, I'm supposed to be your boyfriend, remember?'

She closed her eyes as she hugged him back, savouring the feel of him, the solid, dependable sense of wellbeing he gave her. They'd had no physical contact since the wedding, since she'd turned down his invitation to go home with him, and she'd missed it. Being in his arms gave her a sense of belonging, which was silly because she didn't belong to him, but that was how he made her feel.

'You have perfect timing. Dad's a bit vague with the details. Can you give me a bit more information?' she asked as she stepped backwards, out of his embrace.

Josh was nodding. 'He's had several tests today and the results in most of them were normal but the echocardiogram showed a problem with the mitral valve.'

'You left out that bit of information, Dad,' Georgie reprimanded her father.

'Josh interrupted,' he countered.

'The cardiologist will do some more tests tomorrow to see how serious the problem is. I'll give you a heads up, George, just so you don't get any nasty surprises, but you may need surgery.'

'I thought my arteries were fine and I didn't have a heart attack. Why would I need surgery?'

'The valves in your heart regulate the blood flow. If they're not opening or closing properly, you get insufficient blood pumped around your body and your heart will work harder to compensate for it. That stresses your heart and can lead to a heart attack down the track,' Josh explained. He kept the details simple and Georgie knew her parents would be able to follow his summary. 'The breathlessness and dizziness you've already experienced can be symptomatic of heart disease. But the severity of the symptoms doesn't always indicate the severity of the disease so the cardiologist will investigate further, and that's why I've said you may need surgery. It's a possibility, that's all. Does that make sense?' Josh waited for everyone's agreement before continuing. 'Now George needs to rest and I'm sure you two need to eat,' he said, preparing to bustle them out.

'Well, if you think it's okay to leave him?' Sofia was deferring to Josh.

'You don't need to worry. You can come back in the morning,' he told her.

Her mother turned to Georgie. 'I guess it would be okay to go home. Anastasia offered to cook dinner for us. She's at your house. I hope you don't mind.'

'I don't mind,' she said.

'Have you finished work for the day, Josh?' Sofia asked. 'Would you like to join us?'

Josh looked at Georgie. She tried to keep her face blank; she knew how well he could read her mind. She gave him just the tiniest shake of her head and then held her breath as she waited for his reply. She doubted her parents would be leaving in three days as originally planned and, if that was the case, Josh was going to have to continue to play the part of her boyfriend for a bit longer. But she needed time to digest this thought, they probably both did, and if she was going to survive until her parents left and life returned to normal, she needed to keep everyone in their own little compartments. Which meant only seeing Josh when absolutely necessary. Which meant not tonight.

'Thanks,' he said in response to Sofia's invitation, 'but I've got some other things I need to take care of. I'll catch up with you all again tomorrow. I'm back at QMERT then, but if you have any questions about what's happening speak to the staff here, and if you need further clarification don't hesitate to call me.' He turned to Georgie. 'Are you working tomorrow?'

She nodded and let out the breath she'd been holding.

'I'll see you then,' he said before he left the room.

'Josh?' Georgie called out to him and he turned, stopping in the corridor. She left the room and took a few steps towards him. She reached out, putting one hand on his arm. It was a reflex movement but the moment she touched the bare skin of his forearm and felt the tingle of awareness race through her she realised what she'd done and removed her hand quickly, as though it had been burnt.

'Thank you for taking care of my parents today. Knowing you were here helped when I was stuck out in the chopper.'

He glanced down at his arm, at the spot where her hand had touched him, and when he looked at her his eyes were dark grey, darker than she'd ever seen them before and unfathomable. 'Don't mention it. It was my pleasure. I'll see you tomorrow.'

'Mum and Dad might be here for a bit longer, depending on what dad's tests show. You were expecting to be my surrogate boyfriend for only a couple more days. What do you want to do, what do we say?'

'Don't worry. I'm happy to do this for as long as you need. I won't let you down,' he said. Then he was gone with just a brief nod of his head.

Georgie watched him disappear along the corridor, wondering if he was okay. He seemed upset. She wished she could read his mind as easily as he read hers. She had no idea what could be wrong. She stood looking after him as she tried to figure it out and then realised that nothing was wrong with Josh, something was wrong with her. She was feeling let down because he hadn't kissed her goodbye. She'd come to expect it. But no one had been watching so why should he kiss her?

Her mum joined her and Georgie let her distract her from Josh as they headed for the lifts. 'How are you coping, Mum? This must have come as a bit of a shock.'

'It was quite frightening, not knowing what was wrong. Your dad makes it sound like nothing but, believe me, he looked dreadful. He went quite grey and I thought he wasn't going to make it into the hospital. Thank goodness for Josh,' she said as the lift doors slid open and they stepped inside. 'He was fabulous. He was so good to me, to both of us. He kept checking on me, making sure I knew what was happening. He's quite something, isn't he?'

Georgie kept her gaze averted, avoiding eye contact. She didn't want her mother to read her opinion of Josh on her face, that wouldn't do. Her mother was going to take the news badly when Georgie and Josh had their inevitable 'breakup' and she didn't need her mother to know how much she really liked him—that would only make things harder. 'Mmm,' she replied, hoping that some sort of response would be all that was expected before her mother continued talking.

'I wouldn't have coped nearly so well without him,' Sofia added. 'It's a pity he couldn't join us for dinner.'

Sofia's chatter kept them occupied until they reached the taxi rank and climbed into a cab for the short trip home. Once there, conversation flowed easily between Sofia, Anastasia and Con, and Georgie wasn't required to contribute much at all, which suited her. The others made excuses for her, assuming she must be tired after such a long, exhausting and emotional day, but the reality was that she was quite happy to sit quietly and think about Josh. About how smoothly he'd taken care of all of them, her included. He'd single-handedly turned what could have been an extremely scary, stressful situation into something that seemed manageable. She'd seen his calm, confident approach when they'd worked together but to be on the receiving end of his bedside manner really made her aware of his compassion and ability to read a situation. It appeared that being able to read her mind wasn't his only talent. Her mother was obviously totally impressed by him and it wasn't difficult to see why.

The next few days were a whirlwind of activity, all revolving around her family. The cardiologist determined that George had a diseased mitral valve, which was more serious than his symptoms indicated. He advised George not to fly and advocated immediate valve-replacement surgery, which sent Sofia and Georgie into a spin. In the space of a couple of days George had gone from a fit and active man to one who required heart surgery.

Georgie didn't have many opportunities to think about Josh and their fake relationship, she was too busy concentrating on what her parents needed, but Josh didn't disappear. He worked quietly and tirelessly in the background, taking care of the little tasks that didn't seem important in the bigger picture but still needed to get done. Georgie hadn't asked him to help out but he seemed to be able to sense when things needed to be taken care of, and he did it without any prompting and without seeming to expect any thanks. He was just Josh, doing the things no one else had the time or energy for. He organised for Marty to swap shifts with Georgie so she could keep Sofia company while George was in surgery. He replenished the food in her fridge, filled her car with petrol and even managed to get George and Sofia's flights home to Melbourne changed. Georgie didn't know how he did that, considering he wasn't family, but Louise told her that Josh had gone across to the airport terminal in his QMERT uniform with 'Doctor' embroidered on the chest and had charmed the customer service officer into doing his bidding.

It must have been a female on the counter at the time, Georgie thought, but just picturing the scene made her smile. She didn't care how he'd managed it, she was just grateful for his help. It meant one less thing for her to worry about.

In fact, with Josh's help she found she had very little to worry about. Nothing was too much trouble for him. And it wasn't just Georgie he was taking care of.

He was constantly popping into the hospital to check on her father too. They'd started a regular evening game of backgammon to pass the time and he even helped to entertain Con and Anastasia. His efforts with them gave Georgie more time to spend time with her parents and it was another one of the selfless gestures that benefited her.

She couldn't believe she'd initially wanted to keep their contact to a bare minimum. She now wondered how she would have managed at all over the past few days without his help.

Five days after her dad's surgery Josh and Georgie were in the chopper, heading to Cooktown, two hundred kilometres north of Cairns. Georgie was tired. It had been a stressful few days and while her dad was making a good recovery she was feeling emotionally drained, even with all Josh's help. She'd been trying to keep several balls in the air—updating her brothers, looking after her mother and Con and Anastasia, plus keeping on top of dad's medical condition and working—but Josh had been effectively holding down two jobs and helping her, while somehow managing to remain his usual upbeat, enthusiastic self. Typically for an emergency doctor, he seemed to thrive on challenges. She wasn't quite sure how he'd managed it, but it left her feeling a little incompetent. But things were slowly getting back to normal. Con and Anastasia were leaving today and then it was just a matter of waiting for her dad to recover enough to head home to Melbourne. And then her life would return to normal and she and Josh would go their separate ways.

Georgie didn't actually want to think about that so in an effort to keep her mind occupied with other things she immersed herself in checking the medical kits. She told herself it was imperative that she know exactly what they were carrying, but the reality was that if she kept her head down she didn't need to watch Josh and she knew that's what she would do. It was far safer to sort through the medical kits, even though they didn't need sorting, but she could feel Josh watching her as she worked.

'You've checked that kit three times. Are you going to tell me what's on your mind?' he asked.

'You mean you don't know?' She'd become so used to Josh being able to read her thoughts that to hear him ask her what was wrong was a surprise.

He laughed and the sound cheered her up. 'I could guess but it would be quicker if you told me.'

Georgie flicked the communication switch on her headset to the 'Off' position. She didn't need Pat and Isaac listening to this conversation.

'I'm not sure if I'm ready to go back to Melbourne.'

Josh switched his headset off too before he answered. 'Why don't you stay in Cairns?'

'My parents expect me home and I promised I'd go back at the end of my twelve months. I've always done the right thing but I'm not sure I'm ready to go back to being the Georgie I was when I left. I've changed but I don't know if I've changed enough to avoid slipping back into the role of the dutiful daughter.'

'You'll be all right,' he replied. 'The Georgie I knew first isn't so different from the Georgie I see now. Being you parents' daughter has shaped you into the person you are, someone who embraces other people wholeheartedly and without reservation or judgement. Someone who is compassionate, unselfish, loyal and strong. There is nothing about you that you should want to change.'

'You think I'm strong?'

Josh nodded. 'And capable and confident.'

'I haven't felt very capable this past week. I don't know how I would have managed without your help.'

'You would have been perfectly fine. I didn't do anything you couldn't have done. Have faith in yourself. You can do anything you want to do, be anyone you want to be. Here or in Melbourne.'

Georgie wanted to ask Josh what else he saw in her. What could he see that she couldn't? But Isaac was leaning back between the seats, pointing at his headset, signalling to them to switch their communication on. They flicked the comms switches and Pat's voice came through their headsets. 'There's some rough weather coming—make sure you're buckled in nice and tight.'

The sun disappeared as Georgie checked her harness

and the cabin was cast into semi-darkness. They were over the ocean, heading east away from Cooktown and the Queensland coast. They were searching for a yacht, and were planning to evacuate a sixty-year-old woman who'd slipped and fallen and had a suspected broken leg.

Georgie looked out of the window, lost in her thoughts. Josh saw someone who was strong and confident. She wondered how much of that was due to his influence. She didn't think she would have been nearly as capable over the past week without his help. But perhaps the Georgie she was discovering was those things. She just hoped she could continue to be that person once she was back in Melbourne. Once she was without Josh.

'We should get a visual on the yacht in the next five minutes,' Pat said and as they approached the location they'd been given Isaac, Georgie and Josh all began scanning the ocean for the sailing boat. Away to the west Georgie saw a mass of dark clouds, chasing them over the ocean. The storm was heading their way and she hoped they could outrun it or find the yacht before the bad weather hit.

Ten minutes passed and there was no sign of the yacht. Not one boat could be seen.

'This is Victor Hotel Romeo Hotel Sierra to QMERT Cairns, do you read me?' Pat radioed Louise.

'This is QMERT Cairns, go ahead, Pat.'

'Can we check those coordinates please? I'm overhead now and there's no sign of a yacht.'

Louise read out the coordinates she had been given.

'Confirm that's our current location,' Pat said. 'But, I repeat, I do not have a visual on the yacht. Can you confirm with the vessel and get back to us?'

The clouds were closing in quickly now as Pat circled the chopper over choppy seas while they waited for Louise to confirm the yacht's position.

'QMERT Cairns to Victor Hotel Romeo Hotel Sierra.'

'Go ahead, Lou.'

'I have new coordinates for you, they read them out incorrectly.' Louise relayed the new location and Isaac repeated the coordinates back to her.

'That's thirty nautical miles north-north-west of where we are,' Pat said. 'Please confirm our ETA of fifteen minutes with the vessel and remind them to have their medical assistance flag flying for identification.'

'Will do,' Louise replied.

'This extra flying is going to make fuel pretty tight and the weather's not going to help as we'll be heading into the storm. We'll have to assess the situation when we find the vessel and determine if we can do a safe evacuation.' Pat filled the crew in. Being out over the ocean in bad weather when they were low on fuel was certainly not an ideal position to be in.

'We'll need to be ready to go as quickly as possible,' Georgie told Josh. 'We're not going to have the luxury of time.'

Isaac would lower them to the yacht on a winch. One would go with the stretcher and the medical kits, the other would follow. It was always a tricky manoeuvre as there were so many variables and the weather was only going to complicate matters. They would need to move quickly. 'Let's get the kits strapped onto the stretcher.'

Isaac spotted the yacht on their starboard side as Georgie and Josh finished arranging the equipment. Pat did a flyover and Georgie and Josh peered out the windows.

The sails had all been lowered in preparation for the storm, which had made the yacht more difficult to locate but gave them a good view of the deck. A woman was lying on the lower section of the deck at the foot of a short flight of stairs. They'd expected her to be in the cabin but this was preferable as access was easier. A man was squatting beside her, waving to the chopper.

'I'll go down alone. It'll be faster to evacuate if we only need to do one retrieval,' Josh said.

If only one of them went, it would mean two winch operations instead of four, something that would save precious time.

'That sounds sensible,' Georgie agreed, 'but can you manage to get the patient onto the stretcher on your own?' If the diagnosis was correct and the woman had suffered a broken leg, there was no great need for both of them to attend. The issue wasn't the medical care but the transferring of the woman.

'I should be fine but if it's difficult, her partner will have to lend a hand. If I find things are more complicated than we expected, I'll call you down then.'

Georgie shrugged. 'Okay.'

Isaac was out of his seat and had climbed into the rear of the chopper. He attached all three of them to safety lines.

'The wind is picking up and the forecast is for increasing wind speeds ahead of the storm so we're only going to get one shot at this,' Pat said.

Isaac slid the door open and the wind buffeted them inside the chopper.

'Your call, Josh,' Isaac said.

Georgie watched Josh's face. It was up to him whether he wanted to attempt this evacuation or whether he thought it was too dangerous. His expression was calm, his grey eyes steady and he didn't hesitate.

'Let's do this.'

Josh fastened himself into the harness and together Isaac and Georgie hooked him and the stretcher to the winch before disengaging him from the chopper's safety line.

Isaac directed Pat above the yacht. Pat was flying blind. In order to lower Josh directly onto the yacht, he had to position the chopper above it, meaning he couldn't see either the yacht or Josh on the winch. Isaac became his eyes; he was in charge of the descent. He swung Josh out of the chopper and waited for his signal before he pressed the button and the winch began to lower its load. Josh's head disappeared from view and Georgie watched as he dropped towards the sea.

Georgie was nervous. The yacht looked tiny, bobbing about on the waves beneath them. The sea was rough and it was a difficult exercise; trying to manoeuvre a heavy load on a wire suspended from a moving object onto a moving target was no easy task in calm seas, let alone in rough conditions. Georgie didn't like being in a situation where she had no control. She would have preferred to have been the one going down to the yacht rather than the one sitting, watching and waiting. If she was occupied she wouldn't have time to think of the danger.

Isaac slowed the winch down, trying to get his timing right. He had to lower Josh carefully to avoid crashing him onto the deck if the boat was lifted up on the peak of a wave.

Georgie saw Josh's feet touch the deck, saw him take his weight but then the deck fell away from him as the yacht fell into a trough. Josh was suspended again, his weight hanging on the winch line.

His feet touched the deck for a second time but the yacht tipped. Georgie saw Josh lose his footing and her heart was in her throat as he slipped and fell to his knees. For a second she forgot Josh was securely attached to the chopper, for a second she could imagine him sliding off the yacht into the sea, but then the yacht levelled out and he was on his feet.

He was on the deck now. He'd laid the stretcher out beside him as he knelt and waited for the winch line to give him some slack before unfastening the hook from the strap around his chest. He gave Isaac the signal and Isaac began to pull the cable in as he gave Pat the all-clear to move away, Josh didn't need the downdraught from the chopper to add to the already difficult conditions.

Pat guided the chopper far enough away to avoid the downdraught but close enough to still have visual contact. Georgie could see Josh working quickly, taking observations, talking to the woman's companion, assessing the situation. She wished she'd been able to go with him. Having two of them there would have made his job easier, but the extra time used might have been critical. Neither the weather nor their fuel situation was on their side.

Josh was putting a canula in the woman's vein and, Georgie assumed, giving her something for pain. They had radio communication but there was no need to use it. The others were of no assistance while they were in the chopper but Georgie still wished he'd say something. The silence was making her uneasy.

She saw him quickly splint the woman's leg before rolling her onto her side to get her onto the stretcher. He was working flat out. There was no time to wait for the pain relief to take effect, they needed to get her evacuated and get away from there before the storm hit.

Josh had fastened the straps on the stretcher and was repacking the medical kit. He was kneeling on the deck, his knees spread wide for stability. The woman's partner was bending over the stretcher but was supporting himself against the cabin wall with one hand. The waves had picked up and it seemed he could no longer keep his feet without support.

Josh crawled around to the top of the stretcher to fasten

the protective cage over the woman's face. He was kneeling at her head, reaching for the cage, when a rogue wave slammed into the side of the yacht. The vessel was thrown onto its port side and anything that wasn't tied down went sliding across the deck. Including the stretcher. And Josh.

Georgie watched as though it was happening in slow motion. She saw the woman's partner fall forward, slamming onto the deck. She saw the stretcher sliding towards the sea. She saw Josh's hand on the side of the metal cage.

'Josh!' she yelled, but she was too late. The stretcher had collided with the edge of the deck, trapping Josh's hand. The weight of the stretcher pinned him in place.

CHAPTER NINE

'Josh!'

Georgie didn't know why she was yelling. There was nothing she could do.

Josh was trapped, pinned between the stretcher and the edge of the deck. She could see him trying to pull the stretcher away from the edge but with only one free hand he couldn't apply enough pressure.

The seconds seemed like hours. He needed help. He needed her. She should have been there.

In reality it was only moments before the wave subsided and the yacht righted itself, but the stretcher still didn't move. Josh was still trapped. Georgie could see him trying to shift the weight of it by moving from one leg to the other but because he was kneeling he couldn't get enough force. If the stretcher hadn't been loaded it wouldn't have been a problem, but he had close to one hundred kilograms pinning him to the side of the yacht. He needed help.

What was the other man doing? Georgie looked across the deck. The other man was on his knees and there was blood pouring down his face from a gash on his forehead.

'Isaac, I need to get down there now!' Georgie grabbed a second harness as Pat brought the chopper back over the yacht and Isaac organised the winch.

'Josh, I'm coming down.'

The wind whistled in her ears and her eyes watered as Isaac lowered her to the yacht. She narrowed her eyes, peering down to see how Josh was faring. The waves were tossing the yacht about but the movement of the boat had finally enabled Josh to push the stretcher off his hand. By the time Georgie reached the deck he had locked the protective head cage into place over the stretcher.

'Are you okay?' Georgie asked.

'Yes, I'm fine.' He nodded as he answered, emphasising his point. 'Can you see to Brian?'

The woman's companion, Brian, was now sitting on the deck, looking quite dazed. Blood was still streaming from a cut above his left eye but on examination he didn't seem concussed. Georgie opened a medical kit, looking for swabs, and was cleaning the wound to assess how to treat it when Pat spoke to them from the helicopter.

'Decision time, guys. We've got about fifteen minutes before we need to be heading back for fuel. I can leave now and come back for you but the storm is going to complicate matters. There's no guarantee I'll be able to get back or that we'll be able to get you off the boat. Are you ready to load up now and get out of here?'

Georgie checked Brian again. His head wound wasn't deep, she could see to it on board the chopper but to do so would mean leaving an unmanned yacht bobbing on the Pacific Ocean. Another option was treating Brian and leaving him behind on his own, on a yacht in the middle of a storm. A third option was for one of them to stay behind with Brian.

She looked over at Josh. He was looking pale and she knew he was hurt too. If one of them stayed behind, it would have to be her. She didn't like option two or three.

'I agree we need to get everyone on board the chopper now but what do we do with the yacht?' she asked.

Pat answered. 'I'll alert the coastguard, they'll come out and tow the yacht back.'

'All right,' Georgie replied. 'Let's get going.'

Quickly she taped a dressing over Brian's wound as a temporary fix as she explained to him what was going to happen. She told him to keep some pressure on it and went to help Josh. Isaac was lowering the winch cable and Georgie could see Josh trying to grab it with one hand. Somehow he'd managed to secure one medical kit to the stretcher but he was protecting his left hand, holding it against his chest.

Concern flooded through her. Was he badly injured?

She reached out to him, careful to make sure she didn't knock him off balance. 'Do you need some help? What have you done?'

'I'm okay. It's only a knock to my fingers. We'll worry about it later.'

She didn't have time to argue but she knew he was hurt, which meant they were going to do this evacuation her way. 'You take Brian up first—he's just got a nasty gash on his forehead that'll need stitching—and I'll come up next with the stretcher.'

Josh nodded, surprising her with his easy acquiescence. 'This is Meredith, fractured NOF, no LOC, no other injuries.' Josh gave Georgie a basic summary of Meredith's condition as Georgie fixed a harness around Brian and strapped him to Josh. Isaac winched them to safety and Georgie tried not to watch them every inch of the way.

She attached herself to the stretcher and waited for Isaac to lower the cable for Meredith and herself. Finally, he dragged them into the chopper and the moment they were inside Pat turned for the coast.

Georgie secured the stretcher and she could see Isaac helping to secure Brian and Josh. She wanted to check Josh but he couldn't be her priority. She checked Meredith's vital signs. Her BP and heart rate were slightly elevated but within acceptable limits and her oxygen sats were normal. When she was satisfied that Meredith's condition was stable she attended to Brian. Then, and only then, could she see to Josh.

'Your turn,' she said.

'I'm okay. It's just a couple of fingers.'

He was right, it was only a couple of fingers, but Georgie knew it could have been worse, much worse, and she'd hated the feeling of helplessness and fear that had overcome her. Josh had been in danger and there'd been nothing she could do about it.

'We should have both gone down to the yacht in the first place,' she said, still convinced that somehow she would have been able to keep him safe.

'It was an accident, you couldn't have stopped it,' he replied, still reading her thoughts. She wouldn't have thought she'd smile again today but hearing him voice the words that were in her head made her think everything would be okay.

He was sitting opposite her. She stretched out her hand, reaching for his. He didn't argue any further. He held his left arm out to her. The third, fourth and fifth fingers were already blue and swollen.

'Can you make a fist?' she asked.

He shook his head. 'No.'

She applied gentle pressure across the phalanges of his middle finger. Josh grimaced as she touched the intermediate phalanx. She got the same reaction on his fourth finger.

'Two broken bones, I suspect. Do you want something for the pain?' It had to be hurting regardless of what he told her.

He shook his head. 'No. I don't want anything affecting my judgement. Not while we've got patients on board.'

Georgie could have argued that being in pain could just as easily cloud his judgement but she knew that wasn't the same. 'Okay. I'll strap your fingers for you for now but you'll need to get an X-ray when we get home.'

Josh surrendered his hand again and let Georgie tape his fingers together.

'Georgie?' Pat's voice came through their headsets.

'Yes, Pat.'

'Our fuel's pretty tight. We're going to have to refuel in Cooktown and then head home. Are our patients okay for that?'

'Yes, all three are stable,' Georgie replied with a smile.

It took a long time to get home. Their shift had well and truly ended by then, but fortunately there were no further emergencies. When Pat landed at the hospital Georgie saw an opportunity to get Josh to the radiology department.

'Do you want to go into the hospital? Get your fingers X-rayed before we head to The Sandbar for today's post-mortem?'

He shook his head and made no move to follow the hospital gurneys. 'I'll come back after we knock off.'

'I'll take you, then,' Georgie offered. She wanted to make sure he got seen to. She hadn't been able to prevent the injury but she was going to ensure that he was properly taken care of now. 'I'm going to see Dad before I head to the bar. Mum was going to pick me up but if I drive your car it'll save her the trip.' Georgie knew that if she made it sound as though Josh would be doing someone else a favour he'd be more likely to acquiesce.

Her argument worked and she drove Josh from the QMERT base back to the hospital and delivered him to the radiology department before heading to the cardiology wing.

'Is everything all right, Georgina? You looked exhausted,' Sofia asked her as she entered her father's room.

'Yes, I'm fine,' she told her parents as she kissed them both. 'We just had a rather dramatic day at work,' she said, and proceeded to fill them in on the day's events.

'Do you think this is the right job for you, darling? It sounds terribly dangerous,' Sofia asked once Georgie had finished.

Her parents hadn't loved the idea when she'd told them she was going to retrain as a paramedic and quit nursing, although they had eventually got used to it, but Georgie knew they still had concerns. But ninety per cent of the time the job was routine and risk-free and Georgie loved it. She had no plans to give it up, not even once she was married with kids. But today she'd been frightened, not for herself but watching Josh and being unable to help him had been terrifying. But she didn't tell her parents of her fears neither did she tell them about running low on fuel. The worst hadn't happened, they'd made it home safely, and there was no reason to scare them with hypothetical situations. She was tempted to cross her fingers as she told them, 'I wasn't in any danger today.'

'Well, I'm relieved to hear that,' Sofia said.

Georgie kept her visit brief. She wanted to get to The Sandbar, and she was eager to check on Josh.

Sofia was staying at the hospital to keep George company in Josh's absence but she walked with Georgie to the exit. 'The surgeon had some good news today, darling. He's hoping to discharge your father the day after tomorrow. Dad would like to get home to Melbourne as soon as possible to recuperate there and the surgeon expects to give him medical clearance to fly a day after discharge. Which brings me to a favour I want to ask of you?'

Georgie listened, knowing she was going to agree, but there was one thing she needed to do before she granted her mother's request. And she'd have to do it quickly, as soon as an opportunity presented itself, or perhaps she'd have to create the opportunity. She ran through the possibilities in her head as she walked along the esplanade to The Sandbar.

Josh had beaten her there. He was talking to Isaac and laughing, looking like he didn't have a care in the world. As Georgie watched them, Isaac finished his drink and headed to the bar. Josh was alone.

She went to him. 'How's your hand?'

'Your diagnosis was one hundred per cent correct. Two broken fingers.'

'Are they sore?'

'Not now. I've taken something for that.'

'Are you able to work or do you need some time off?'

'I'm fine. I'm going to go into the physio department tomorrow and get a proper splint made. That should take care of things while they heal. It's no big deal.'

No big deal. He had been lucky to escape with just two broken fingers. Georgie remembered how she'd felt as the yacht had tipped on its side. She'd been terrified it was going to go over. Terrified it was about to drop Josh into the ocean. She had no idea whether capsizing a boat was easy to do, she hadn't had much experience with boats, but she did know she'd never been as frightened as she had been then.

It was time to face facts. There was no point denying that Josh sent her crazy with desire. That the touch of his hand sent her hormones wild, that his smile made her heart race or that his kisses made her want to leap into bed with him. She did. And sometimes it felt like it was all she could think about. She wanted Josh and if she didn't do something about it now, tonight, she was going to miss her opportunity. She hadn't forgotten how it felt to be in his embrace and she was having a hard time letting that memory go.

The team was celebrating the safe evacuation and return to Cairns but to Georgie tonight was about more than that. Tonight was about Josh.

'You haven't got a drink. Can I get you something?' he asked, seeing her empty hands.

It was now or never. 'That depends,' she said.

'On what?'

'On whether or not you're ready to go home.'

Josh looked at his watch. His left hand and fingers, what she could see of them where they emerged from the strapping, were swollen and bruised. 'But you just got here and it's still early,' he said.

'I know. But I thought I'd come home with you.' She looked up at him through her lashes and gave him a half-smile. She saw him read between the lines.

'Just the two of us?' he asked.

She licked her lips and smiled fully now. 'I thought that might be fun,' she said.

'Why now?'

Had she missed her chance already? Had he changed his mind? Given up?

'I'm tired of trying to fight this attraction,' she admitted. 'It's not going away. Pretending it doesn't exist hasn't worked. Ignoring it hasn't worked. I can't pretend I don't want you. I want to know what it's like to make love with you. I want to know how it feels. I've never seen the point in spending just one night with someone but it was so hard today, watching you in danger, and I realised that one chance, one night, is all I might have, and I know I'll regret it if I don't take it.'

'Are you sure?'

'This is what I want. No strings. No promises. Just this night.'

'But—'

'I know our relationship is an illusion,' she interrupted. 'I know it's not real and I don't expect a real relationship but you were right, our chemistry is real and all I'm asking for is just one night. You've taught me to take chances. You've given me the confidence to try new things. This is something I want. But if you're not feeling up to it…?' She let the question tail off into thin air.

Josh grinned at her, his grey eyes shining with excitement. 'A couple of busted fingers won't slow me down.' He drained his drink in one swallow and put his glass on a table. 'Ready when you are.'

'Down, boy.' Georgie laughed. 'Meet me out the front in five minutes. I don't want everyone to see us leaving together. They don't need any more fuel added to the fire of speculation.'

Georgie went to the ladies' bathroom to freshen up. Beside the hand dryer, directly opposite the door, was a condom vending machine. It was the first thing she saw as she walked in. She crossed the room and stood in front of it. She studied it. Was she really going to do this?

It would just be one night, she told herself. It didn't have to change anything.

She couldn't deny she'd spent many hours imagining just what it would be like. There was nothing stopping her. Nothing would change except she would know how it felt to let Josh love her.

She turned to her right and looked in the mirror. Her eyes were dark and shining. Her cheeks were flushed and her lips were bright red. Her blood vessels were dilating in anticipation. She wanted this.

She searched her purse for coins and inserted them into the machine. She twisted the knob and caught the little packet as the machine dispensed it and she stashed it in her handbag. She wanted this more than she'd wanted anything in a long time.

She left the bathroom and went to meet Josh.

He was waiting under a palm tree, leaning against the trunk looking calm and relaxed. She was a bundle of nerves. It had been a long time since she'd been intimate with a man, but she wasn't apprehensive. She was excited. She reached for his right hand and pulled him away from the tree.

'Are—?'

'Shh.' Georgie pressed her fingers against his lips. She didn't want to talk, she didn't want a discussion, she just wanted to get to Josh's apartment and make love.

Josh had left his car at the hospital and they didn't speak as they walked. The heat from Josh's hand was searing her palm, threatening to ignite her entire body. She could imagine how his hands would feel running over her naked skin, how her body would respond to his touch.

He pressed the button for the lift and Georgie was grateful he lived so close to The Sandbar. She didn't think she could make it much further. He held the door for her and followed her into the empty lift, pushing the button for the seventh floor on his way past. She stood in the corner and pulled him to her. She wasn't going to wait any longer. This was part of her fantasy. This was what tonight was about, satisfying her curiosity and their desire.

She reached her arm up and cupped her hand around the back of his head, guiding his mouth to hers. She kissed him hard and he kissed her back. His hands were on her hips, holding her to him. Her hands were behind his head, keeping him with her.

She felt the lift stop, heard the doors open. She didn't care if more people were getting into the lift, she didn't care if they were surrounded, she had no space in her head for thoughts of anyone else.

Josh was holding her hand, pulling her out of the lift. They were at the seventh floor. He unlocked his apartment door and they turned left, heading for the bedroom, not pretending this was about anything more than desire, lust and longing.

Georgie dropped her bag on the bed and went straight back into Josh's arms. She ran her hands under his shirt. She trailed her fingernails lightly over his skin and heard him moan. She grabbed the bottom of his shirt and pulled it over his head, exposing his flat, toned stomach. He started to undo his belt but Georgie stopped him.

'Let me,' she said. It would be difficult for him to undress with three fingers strapped together, though not impossible, but Georgie wanted the pleasure of doing it. She undid his belt and snapped open the button on his pants before sliding the zip down. She could feel the hard bulge of his erection pressing into her, straining to get free.

Josh stepped out of his shoes, not bothering to untie the laces, as she pushed his trousers to the floor. His pants joined his shoes and shirt in an untidy heap. He was naked except for his boxer shorts. Georgie looked him over.

He was glorious.

CHAPTER TEN

HE GRINNED at her and raised one eyebrow. In reply she put a hand on his smooth, broad chest and pushed him backwards until the bed bumped the back of his knees and made him sit. It was his turn to wait for her now.

She picked up her bag and opened it. Retrieving the condom, she placed it on the bedside table. Josh watched every move she made.

She stepped back from the bed. Out of his reach. He could watch but he couldn't touch. She wanted to tease him. She reached for the zip at the side of her dress and undid it slowly. She slipped one strap from her shoulder and then the other and let the dress fall to the floor. Josh's eyes were dark grey now, all traces of silver vanishing as he watched and waited for her.

She reached her hands behind her back and unhooked her bra, sliding it along her arms and dropping it to the floor. She lifted her hand to pull the elastic from her hair.

'Let me do that.' Josh's voice was husky with desire. Lust coated his words, making them so heavy they barely made it past his lips.

Georgie dropped her hand, leaving her hair restrained. She slid her underwear from her hips and went to him. She was completely naked but she didn't feel exposed. She felt powerful.

She sat on the bed beside him. He reached for her with his right hand, running it up her arm. His fingers rested at the nape of her neck before he flicked her plait over her left shoulder and pulled the elastic from her hair. He wound his fingers through her hair, loosening the plait as he spread her hair out, letting it fall over her shoulders before burying his face in it.

His thumb rested on her jaw. It was warm and soft, his pressure gentle. He ran his thumb along the line of her jaw and then replaced it with his lips. He kissed her neck, her collarbone and the hollow at the base of her throat.

His fingers blazed a trail across her body that his mouth followed. Down from her throat to her sternum, over her breast to one nipple. His fingers flicked over the nipple, already peaked and hard. His mouth followed, covering it, sucking, licking and tasting.

He pulled her backwards onto the bed.

She reached for his boxer shorts and pulled them from his waist. His erection sprang free, pressing against her stomach.

His fingers were stroking the inside of her thigh. She parted her legs and his fingers slid inside her, into her warm, moist centre. His thumb rolled over her most sensitive spot, making her gasp. He kissed her breast, sucking at her nipple as his thumb teased her. She arched her back, pushing her hips and breasts towards him, wanting more, letting him take her to a peak of desire.

Still she wanted more. She needed more.

She rolled towards him and pushed him flat onto his back. She sat up and straddled his hips. His erection rose between them, trapped between their groins. Georgie stretched across him, reaching for the condom, and her breasts hung above his face. He lifted his head, taking her breast into his mouth once more. She closed her eyes as she gave herself up to the sensations shooting through her as his tongue flicked over her nipple. Every part of her responded to his touch. Her body came alive under his fingers and his lips and her skin burned where their bodies met.

She felt for the condom, finding it with her fingers. She picked it up and lifted herself clear of Josh, pulling her breast from his lips. Air flowed over her nipple, the cool temperature contrasting with the heat of his mouth. She opened the condom and rolled it onto him. Her fingers encircled his shaft as she smoothed out the sheath.

She put her hands either side of his head and kept her eyes on his face as she lifted herself up and took him inside her. His eyelids closed and she watched him breathe in deeply as her flesh encased him, joining them together.

She filled herself with his length before lifting her weight from him and letting him take control. His thumbs were on the front of her hips, his fingers behind her pelvis as he guided her up and down, matching her rhythm to his thrusts, each movement bringing her closer to climax.

She liked this position. She liked being able to watch him, she liked being able to see him getting closer and closer to release. His eyes were closed, hiding their silver flecks, but his lips were parted, his breathing was rapid and shallow, his thrusts getting faster.

She spread her knees, letting him in deeper inside her until she had taken all of him. Her body was flooded with heat. Every nerve ending was crying out for his touch. 'Now, Josh. Now.'

He opened his eyes and his grey gaze locked with hers as he took her to the top of the peak.

Her body started to quiver and she watched him as he too shuddered. He closed his eyes, threw his head back and thrust into her, claiming her as they climaxed together.

When they were spent she lay on him, covering his body with hers. Their skin felt warm and flushed from their effort and they were both panting as he wrapped his arms around her back, holding her to him. She could feel his heart beating under her chest. She could feel it as its rhythm slowed, gradually returning to normal.

'Wow.'

Josh's prediction had been right. Their chemistry made for amazing sex. Georgie had never been so overwhelmed by an experience. It was a pity she wasn't going to be able to get used to it.

'Wow indeed,' he said as he kissed her shoulder. 'Do you think we could improve on that with practice?'

Georgie laughed. 'I'm not sure it gets much better than that.'

'Give me a minute and we'll see.'

A minute! She needed longer to recover than that. 'I can't stay. Mum was expecting me home after dinner.'

'We haven't had dinner,' he said.

'She doesn't know that.'

Josh's fingers were running along her spine and Georgie would have been more than happy to stay right where she was. But that wasn't part of her plan. She didn't want to go, she wanted to spend the night in Josh's arms and forget about the world, but she couldn't stay. The longer she stayed, the harder it would be to make herself leave.

Tonight was about the present. It was a once-in-a-lifetime opportunity. They didn't have a future. She would have her memories but she wouldn't have Josh.

God, she was a fool, she thought later as she climbed into her own bed. Her sheets were cold and clean. They smelt of detergent and sunshine but she wanted them to smell of

Josh. She never should have slept with him. Now she had to walk away from the best sex of her life.

But it shouldn't matter. Great sex was just great sex. She could appreciate it for what it was and move on. Great sex wasn't a basis for a lasting relationship and that was what she wanted, the one thing Josh couldn't give her.

She was looking for a relationship based on respect, shared values and companionship, not on great sex; but she knew that, at the moment, she'd trade respect and shared values for another night with Josh.

Josh wasn't at work the following day as he had a physio appointment but he arrived at the hospital for his regular game of backgammon with her father just as she was leaving. He was waiting for her in the corridor.

He was wearing jeans and a green T-shirt, his hair was spiky and he looked just as he'd looked last night when she'd left him all rumpled in his bed. The only difference was that he was dressed and the fingers of his left hand were encased in a splint.

He was smiling at her. She wanted to tell him to stop, it was messing with her equilibrium and with her resolve, but she couldn't speak—her mouth was dry, her knees were weak and her heart was racing. Her body reacted even before her brain had fully registered that he was there. Last night couldn't be repeated. They wouldn't share another night. She'd have to get over it but her body seemed to have other ideas.

'Hi. I was hoping I'd catch you here.' He stepped towards her and reached for her hand. His eyes were dark grey but as their hands touched she saw silver flecks flash in his irises like little lightning strikes and she felt the flash race through her. 'Can you sneak away tonight?' he asked.

No, she meant to say, but when she opened her mouth to speak that wasn't the word that came out. 'Yes,' she said.

'My place? Eight-thirty?'

She nodded and tried to tell herself that when she got there she'd explain why she couldn't stay, why they couldn't have another night. But then Josh leant forward and kissed her lips and she felt her resolve crumble into a pool of rampant desire.

She smelt of cinnamon and honey. He closed his eyes and savoured her scent as he kissed her in the hospital corridor. In ninety minutes she would be in his arms once again but first he had an appointment to keep.

'Evening, George,' he said as he entered the room. George was sitting out of bed, looking a picture of health, but the room was bare. The flowers, cards and magazines that had been cluttering all the horizontal surfaces of his room and giving it some personality were gone. 'What's going on?' he asked as he looked around.

'I'm being discharged in the morning,' George explained.

'That's great news.'

George was nodding. 'I'll be glad to get home, that's for sure. This wasn't how I planned to spend my holiday. Not that I'm complaining, it could have been a lot worse, it could have been my last one.' George stood and crossed to the table and picked up a small case that was lying there. It was his backgammon set and it was the only personal item that hadn't already been packed away. 'Have you got time for one final game?'

'Of course,' Josh said, 'but I'll warn you now, this time I'm going to win.'

George laughed. 'Give it your best shot, but if you couldn't beat me when I was medicated up to my eyeballs following surgery, I don't fancy your chances now.' He flipped the catches on the case and opened it out, quickly positioning the checkers. They sat on the edge of the bed, the table between them, and started to play. As had become their habit, Josh went first.

'You've been given medical clearance to fly?' he asked as he shook his dice in their cup and rolled them out.

'Yep. I had another echocardiogram today and a stress test and apparently it's all looking like it should. I've got my piece of paper and the flights are all booked. I was a bit nervous about flying but the specialist says it's fine and Georgie's coming home with us.'

Josh was about to move his checkers but he hesitated. 'Georgie's going with you?'

George was watching the board, waiting for Josh's move, but he looked up quickly. 'She hasn't told you?'

Josh shook his head, afraid to hear what George would say next.

'She's taking holidays and coming home.' George threw his dice as he spoke.

Josh didn't like the sound of that. 'So she's coming back?'

'I'm not sure. You'd have to ask her,' George said as he moved his checkers. 'What are your plans? You're only in Cairns temporarily too, I understand. What's next for you?'

Josh wondered if it was a deliberate change in the direction of conversation. Was there more George wasn't telling him? But George had always called a spade a spade and Josh couldn't imagine him keeping something from him now. 'I'm waiting to hear about an appointment at Brisbane General,' he answered.

'For what position?'

'Head of Emergency.'

'That sounds important.'

'I've been working towards a position like this for years. As you can imagine, they don't come up all that often. The current head of emergency suggested I come to Cairns to get some more experience in emergency retrievals. He's due to retire when I finish here and I'm hoping to be able to step into his role. That's where I'm headed.'

'You've no plans to come to Melbourne?' George asked.

Josh shook his head, aware that George was watching him closely. 'No.'

'Georgie knows of your career plan?'

'She does,' Josh replied, thinking that he'd at least been honest with her about his future direction. He wondered when, or if, she was going to tell him about her departure and whether or not she was planning on returning.

'Well, if you ever find yourself in Melbourne, be sure to come and see us,' George said as he moved his last checker into the home position, victorious in yet another game of backgammon. 'You'll always be welcome.'

It was close to midnight and Josh knew Georgie would be going home soon. All evening he'd been waiting for her to tell him about her plans to return to Melbourne but she'd said nothing. Not before or after they'd made love. They were lying in his bed, naked. He knew his bed would feel cold and empty when she left. She was tucked in against his shoulder. He had his arm around her and the top of her head was resting under his chin. Her skin was soft under his hand and he was surrounded by the scent of honey and cinnamon. He closed his eyes and let her scent invade his senses. He could get used to this.

No. He didn't want to get used to this. That was a dangerous thought.

He needed to keep his defences up. He had to get on

with his future. He couldn't get caught up in Georgie. Her parents would be returning to Melbourne and his life would return to normal. While he had enjoyed this interlude, it was only ever going to be temporary. That was their arrangement and that was the way he operated. He would keep his memories but he would move on.

He opened his eyes and moved his head slightly so that Georgie's head was no longer under his chin, trying to avoid her scent of honey and cinnamon so he could concentrate. 'Your dad told me he's going to be discharged tomorrow. That's good news.'

She nodded.

'And you're going home with them?' Josh asked, even though he already knew the answer. What he didn't know was what would happen next and it seemed that unless he asked, he was never going to find out.

'He wants to go home to Melbourne to recuperate but he's nervous about flying. They've asked me to fly with them,' she explained.

'When will you be back?'

'I'm not coming back.'

Josh frowned and wondered if that's what George had been keeping from him. 'What do you mean? You've still got another month on your contract.'

'I've applied to take annual leave. We leave the day after tomorrow.'

He'd known she was leaving, just as he was, but he hadn't expected it to be so soon. He'd thought she'd come back, give them time to say their goodbyes. He was ready to move on but he hadn't expected to start the process tonight.

He tried to be pleased. He should be pleased. Surely this was a good thing.

* * *

Georgie was lying in Josh's arms. She'd hoped to resist him but it had been impossible to forego her one last opportunity. He'd opened his apartment door for her and kissed her senseless before he'd started undressing her with his eyes, and she known then she'd end up here, naked, in his bed. He hadn't needed to say a word. In fact, he hadn't spoken, he'd just looked at her and her heart had pounded so hard in her chest she'd thought it would explode. Her hands had been shaking as he'd held them and pulled her to him. She'd stepped into his arms and kissed him, followed him to his bed and made love to him. Now she was lying in his arms, her head nestled in the curve of his shoulder, her cheek resting on his bare chest, her ear pressed against his heart, listening to it beating.

His words vibrated in his chest when he spoke, reverberating under her ear. It wasn't quite where she'd planned to have the conversation about leaving Cairns, leaving him, but he'd opened the discussion and she couldn't put it off any longer. She didn't have any more time.

'I've applied to take annual leave. We leave the day after tomorrow.' Accompanying her parents on the flight back to Melbourne was the favour her mum had asked of her and it had given her the perfect escape clause. And she was going to take it. She knew she had to get away from Josh quickly before it became impossible. She was going to Melbourne and she wasn't coming back. She'd decided that the way to get over Josh was to have a quick, clean break.

'So that's it? You're leaving now?'

'It's only a bit earlier than I'd planned. It's not going to make any difference in the scheme of things.'

She wanted Josh to tell her that it would make a difference to him. She wanted him to ask her to come back. Or not to go. But of course he didn't. She was a fool to hope for that. He didn't want a relationship, he'd told her that. 'Your life can return to normal. No more pretending,' she said.

'I thought…'

'What?'

He shook his head and she could feel his shoulders shaking with the movement. 'Never mind.' He paused briefly and she was left wondering what he'd been going to say. 'So what was last night all about? And tonight?' he asked.

'It was about you. Us.' She shrugged. 'Your philosophy has rubbed off on me. I was being adventurous. This was sex with no strings attached. That was what you wanted.'

He didn't argue.

She wished he would.

But he didn't protest and as she lay in his arms she knew he would keep quiet. He wasn't going to beg her to stay.

What on earth had she expected? Had she thought he was going to tell her he loved her and he couldn't live without her?

She'd made a mess of everything. She should have left him alone. She should never have crossed the invisible line they'd drawn. But she hadn't been able to resist.

The old Georgie would have resisted. The old Georgie hadn't had casual sex but she knew that was also true of the new Georgie. She was kidding herself if she thought going to bed with Josh could be considered casual sex. She'd known exactly what she was doing. The question was, why had she done it? Why had she crossed that invisible line?

And she knew the answer too. She'd crossed the line both physically and emotionally.

She'd fallen in love with him.

She had come to Cairns to find her independence. To find herself. She hadn't expected to fall in love but that's what had happened. She had begun the process of her metamorphosis from dutiful daughter to independent woman; she'd engineered the move away from home; and Josh had helped her to complete it. He'd helped to complete her. She was now the person she wanted to be but would she be able to continue to be that person without Josh by her side?

She would have to do it, she thought, she had no other option. But that meant the sooner she got away from here the better, before she lost herself in Josh.

She was leaving for Melbourne tomorrow. Part of her couldn't believe it. She knew she would find it hard to leave but she had no other option. She'd told everyone of her decision and nothing had happened to change her mind. Or, more specifically, no one had tried to convince her to stay.

Her last shift with QMERT was an ordinary day. She was working with Sean and they were called out for a couple of routine inter-hospital transfers, nothing dramatic, nothing difficult. Without realising it, she'd shared her last shift with Josh the day they'd evacuated Meredith and Brian from the yacht off the coast of Cooktown. But she would see him tonight. She was on her way to The Sandbar for her farewell dinner and drinks, and Josh would join them there after his hospital shift.

This was going to be the last time she saw him and she was determined to put on a happy face. She was trying to be brave. Trying to pretend she was happy to be going home. Pretending she was ready. Pretending she didn't mind that he hadn't asked her to stay. Or come back.

Pretending she hadn't fallen in love.

But, of course, nothing in the world of emergency medicine ever went to plan when she needed it to.

Her mobile rang as she walked into the bar and Josh's name appeared on her screen. As she answered she could hear sirens in the street. This was only going to be bad news.

'Georgie, it's me. I've been held up. There's been a fire at one of the backpacker hostels and it's all hands on deck while we wait to see what the ambos bring us. I have no idea yet how bad it is or how long I'll be.'

Disappointment surged through her but there was nothing she could do. 'It's okay.'

'I'm sorry. I really wanted to be there.'

'I understand, Josh. I know how it goes. Hopefully we'll see you later.'

She would have a drink with her other colleagues but Josh was the one she really wanted to see. The night dragged from that point on.

She waited and waited but Josh didn't show. She checked her mobile phone constantly but it was hours before she heard it beep, signalling a text message. She pulled it out of her handbag.

Can't get away. Working at QMERT 2mro, will c u at terminal.

'Is something wrong?' Louise was standing beside her. 'You've been looking at your phone every five minutes.'

'Everything's fine,' she lied. 'That was Josh, he's still at the hospital. I was waiting to see him, to say goodbye, but if he's not going to make it I think I might go home. There are still some things I need to do before we leave tomorrow.' That wasn't true either. She'd packed and the removalists had collected her boxes and her car. All she had to do was get up and go to the airport but she didn't want to be at the bar any longer without Josh.

'I'll give you a lift home,' Louise offered. 'It's past my bedtime too.'

Louise drove down the esplanade and along the sea-front. 'We're going to miss you,' she said as she drove. 'You've been a breath of fresh air around the place.'

'I'm going to miss all of you too. I've loved my time here,' Georgie replied, but her heart was heavy with the knowledge that there was one person she was going to miss most.

'Why don't you come back?' Louise asked as they passed the hospital.

Georgie couldn't help looking through the emergency entrance, hoping for a glimpse of Josh, but of course she saw nothing except for a couple of paramedics standing by their ambulance. Her heart ached in her chest, knowing that Josh was just a few metres from her but unreachable.

'Because there's nothing for me here,' she answered. Josh was leaving too, there was nothing to bring her back to Cairns. She sighed with longing and the sound escaped from her and broke the silence.

Louise slowed the car and turned her head to watch Georgie. 'Did you want to go in and say goodbye?'

Georgie looked at her, wondering how much she thought she knew. 'No, he'll be busy.'

'I'm sure he'll stop for you.'

Georgie didn't think so. She shook her head.

'Have you told him how you feel?'

Georgie heard her own sharp intake of breath. 'What do you mean?'

'Marty was right about the two of you, wasn't he? Your relationship isn't pretend any more,' Lou said. 'Does Josh know how you feel?'

Georgie didn't bother denying Lou's assessment but she wasn't about to announce it to everyone and especially not to Josh. 'No. And I won't tell him.'

'What if he feels the same way? What if both of you are too stubborn to be the first to admit your feelings?'

She wished she was brave enough to take that chance but although she was more confident than she'd been a year ago, she wasn't that brave. 'He has a totally different view of it. He doesn't want a proper relationship.'

'He's a man,' Lou scoffed with the voice of experience. 'I doubt he has any idea what he really wants. You need to tell him.'

'No.'

Louise turned the corner and the hospital receded into the distance. 'Have you thought about moving to Brisbane? You'd get a job there.'

Georgie shook her head again.

'Why not?'

'Because Josh hasn't asked me to.' She knew it wouldn't take more than that to get her to pack her bags and move again. All he had to do was ask. But that wasn't going to happen. 'It's okay, Lou, I'm okay,' she said before her friend felt she had to offer counselling. 'Josh and I had a deal. This whole thing was make-believe, I just forgot that temporarily.'

To her relief Louise didn't question her further. She probably realised that Georgie had a point. No matter what she or Louise thought, there wasn't anything they could do to change the situation. It was what it was. Life would go on. Without Josh.

Georgie had made it through her last night in Cairns by consoling herself with the idea she'd see Josh at the airport before she left. He'd told her he'd get across to the airport terminal. She wanted to know she would see him one last time, it would make it easier to leave, but as the taxi drove her and her parents along the entry road she saw the helicopter taking off from the QMERT base. Her heart sank in her chest. Josh would be on board, on his way to an emergency, which meant he wouldn't be meeting her at the terminal. He wouldn't be saying goodbye.

Disappointment and frustration left a bitter taste in her mouth. She'd prepared herself to say goodbye but she hadn't prepared herself not to.

Perhaps it was for the best, she thought as she started piling luggage onto the trolley. There was always the danger that if she saw him again she might just tell him she'd fallen in love with him. And there was no need for him to know that. It was better this way. She needed to move on.

CHAPTER ELEVEN

IT WAS a glorious spring day in Melbourne. One of those perfect days that made up for the many bleak, grey wintry days the city seemed to exist on. Or perhaps that was her perception. In the two months since Georgie had been back in Melbourne every day had seemed grey and wintry.

Today was her parents' fortieth wedding anniversary, a day her parents had been looking forward to celebrating, but she was having trouble mustering up any enthusiasm. She was pleased for her parents but every time a wedding was mentioned it just served to remind her of her own situation.

She was still single but dating, and for the past few weeks had been seeing Con and Anastasia's son Michael. She knew Michael was more into the whole idea than she was and it was getting to the stage where she'd have to do something about that. She knew everyone was hoping for some sort of announcement and while he was nice enough they had no chemistry, no spark. Maybe that would come, but all she could think of was the instant connection she'd had with Josh. He'd been a perfect stranger yet they'd had an immediate, physical attraction, an awareness, a connection, and it hadn't dissipated. If she was honest, it was still overpowering her, making everything else seem paler, less significant, weaker.

She couldn't bring herself to get excited about anything at the moment. Least of all Michael. But that wasn't his fault. She wanted Josh and she couldn't imagine wanting anyone else the same way.

Georgie knew she should be focussing on her future. Josh was history. She hadn't heard from him since she'd arrived back in Melbourne but it was proving impossible to forget about him.

'Are you looking forward to dinner tonight?' Sofia asked her as they sat at the hairdresser together. The official party that had originally been planned to celebrate the anniversary had been replaced with a small dinner for the immediate family due to George's surgery. The big celebration would now take place in two weeks' time but Sofia had decided that a family dinner was enough of an occasion to warrant a trip to the beautician and the hair salon.

Georgie looked across at her mother. Today was such a special occasion for her that she would have to try, at least, to pretend to be happy. 'Of course.'

'Are you sure you don't want to invite Michael? You know he's welcome.'

'I'm positive. It will be nice to have dinner with just the family. I feel like I still haven't caught up with all the boys properly since I got home from Cairns,' Georgie said, making excuses. 'Michael doesn't need to come.'

She could feel her mother's watchful gaze on her but she avoided eye contact. 'How are things going with him?'

'Fine.'

'What does that mean exactly?'

Georgie didn't need to look at her mother to know she'd raised her eyebrows and was giving her a questioning look. 'Fine means fine. It means there are no problems, no dramas. There's no anything really.' She sighed.

There was a brief silence and Georgie knew her mother was weighing up her next words. 'Can I ask you a question? When you picture your own fortieth wedding anniversary, who do you see by your side?'

Georgie didn't respond. She didn't know what to say. How honest to be.

Sofia didn't wait for an answer. 'It's not Michael, is it?'

Georgie shook her head.

'Is it Josh?' Sofia asked.

She risked a glance at her mother. 'Why do you ask?'

'For the twenty-seven years that I've been lucky enough to be your mother I've never seen you look like you do when Josh is around. You glow from within, as though something about him gives you an extra boost, makes you complete. Are you in love with him?'

Georgie swallowed hard. 'It doesn't matter if I am. We don't have a future together.'

'What makes you say that?'

'He doesn't want to get married. He doesn't want a relationship. His future is about his career.' Hot tears gathered in her eyes as she remembered that Josh hadn't chosen her. 'His dream is to be head of the emergency team at Brisbane General. His dream isn't me.'

'Have you heard from him?'

Georgie shook her head.

'It's going to make it difficult for you to find someone while you're still in love with Josh.'

'I'll get over him.' She was not going to admit to her mother that she was right. It wasn't going to do her any good to acknowledge her feelings. She wished she was brave enough to admit she loved him, but the confidence that Josh had seen in her, the confidence he believed she had, seemed to have forsaken her. Somehow he'd helped her believe in herself. 'I don't want to spend the rest of my life alone. I'm sure you and Dad can find someone for me, seeing as I haven't done a very good job of that myself. Maybe an arranged marriage isn't such a bad idea. It worked for you.'

'Ours was a slightly different proposition.'

Georgie frowned. 'What do you mean?'

'Our families came to Australia from the same village in Greece. Your father and I practically grew up together, but when we fell in love we decided the best way to ensure that we were able to get married was to let your grandparents believe they were arranging our marriage.'

'You fell in love and then got married?' This version of the story was different from the one Georgie had grown up hearing.

Sofia was nodding. 'Your father sowed the seeds of the idea and then we let our parents work it out. That arrangement suited everybody. We all got what we wanted. Your grandparents believed they had final approval and your dad and I got each other. Your father wants to see you settled and happy but we don't want you getting married because we think it's the right thing for you to do. We would never encourage you to marry someone you don't love. We want you to be happy.'

Georgie wanted to be happy again too, but right now she was miserable. She wanted to feel complete but she knew that was impossible. She'd gone to Cairns on a mission to find herself. The irony was Josh had helped her to discover her true self, but she couldn't maintain it without him. She needed him. Part of her had remained behind with Josh and she knew she'd never be complete again without him.

Josh took the coffee pot off the stove as he tried not to think about the free Saturday that stretched emptily in front of him. It was the first free day he'd had in the past eighteen since he'd moved back to Brisbane General to take up his new position as Head of Emergency. The role had been offered to him earlier than expected and he'd jumped at the chance. Not only was it the job he wanted but it gave him a reason to leave Cairns.

He'd thought leaving Cairns was the answer. He'd thought it would help him get his life back in control. After all, taking up this position meant he was achieving his goals. And leaving Cairns should help him to forget about Georgie. It would remove him from everything they had in common, from all the familiar places they'd shared. But, of course, he took his memories with him and even taking on the new job didn't keep him busy enough to forget about her.

Last weekend he'd chosen to spend his days at the hospital, finding his feet, he'd told himself, rather than spending the days alone. His own company wasn't something he normally minded but he wasn't particularly enjoying his solitude at the moment. He wasn't particularly enjoying anything.

He thought about what he'd shared with Georgie—sex with no strings attached. It was what he'd asked for and what he'd been given, but it hadn't been the answer either. Too late he'd discovered that it wasn't what he truly wanted. He wanted the strings. He missed the strings.

The phone rang, interrupting his sombre thoughts. He recognised the QMERT Cairns number as he answered.

'Hi, Josh, it's Lou. How are you? How's Brisbane? How's the new job?' In typical Lou fashion she barely paused for breath.

'Good.'

There was silence. Josh had expected her to jump straight in with her next question but she was obviously waiting for him to elaborate and he had nothing more to say. The job was good, it was everything he'd expected, but it wasn't enough. He had the job he wanted but he didn't have the girl. And he wasn't about to tell Louise that.

'I've got some mail here for you.'

Louise had his forwarding address. Why was she ringing to tell him about random mail?

'It's from Georgie's parents,' she said. 'I got one too. It's an invitation to their fortieth wedding anniversary celebrations. I'll send it down to you.'

'Thanks. When's the party?'

'In two weeks,' Lou said. 'But why did they send the invitation here? Don't they know you're in Brisbane? Haven't you spoken to Georgie?'

Ah, her phone call made more sense now. 'No. Why would I have?'

'I just thought you might have called to tell her you'd got the job and were back in Brisbane. I'm sure she would be pleased for you.'

'Have you spoken to her?' he asked. Maybe Louise could tell him what he wanted to know. 'Is she—?' He cut himself off. He couldn't ask the questions he wanted to. Is she seeing anyone? Is she happy? It wasn't up to Louise to tell him the answers. Lou was right, he should have called Georgie himself. But he couldn't do that. Somehow that would feel as if he'd be losing control. He changed his words. 'Is she enjoying being back in Melbourne?'

'I think she's taking some time to settle back in. You should call her, tell her you'll go down to Melbourne for the party.'

'No. I don't think I will.'

'Why not? I thought you'd want to catch up with her. I still don't understand why you let her go.'

'Because I'm not the man she's looking for. I'm not what she needs.'

'Did she tell you that?' He could hear the surprise in Lou's voice.

'No. She didn't need to. I'm not cut out for relationships, for commitment. I'm no good at it.'

'What a load of rubbish. You've obviously just never been in the right relationship.'

'My relationships always end in disaster. She's better off without me.'

'There's always the chance that the two of you would be better off together than apart. Georgie wants someone to love. What if that someone was you? Have you thought about that? Unless, of course, you're happy alone?'

No, he wasn't happy, he thought as he hung up the phone, but being alone meant having complete control over his life.

But he didn't feel like he was in control of anything. His career was supposed to be all he needed but it was no longer enough.

He missed her.

He wanted to know how she was. He wanted to hear about her day. He wanted to be able to come home and share his day with her.

But he had his reasons for not calling. He'd been speaking the truth when he'd told Lou he was no good at relationships. Georgie wanted a happy ending and she wasn't going to get it from him. It was better for him to be miserable and alone than to make Georgie miserable.

But he missed her.

And she wasn't coming back. She was hundreds of miles away from him. Waiting for someone else to sweep her off her feet.

The realisation hit him that this was it. This was going to be his life. Georgie wasn't coming back to him. He hadn't really imagined what his life was going to be like without her. He couldn't imagine it.

But what if she loved him like he loved her? What then?

He loved her.

He was an idiot.

He loved her.

Why hadn't he realised that?

Why did love always make such a fool of him?

The first time he'd been in love, Tricia and his brother had made a fool of him. This time he was doing it without help from anyone else. But this time it wasn't too late. Or so he hoped. He loved Georgie and this time he had a chance to change the outcome.

Georgie wanted to fall in love. What if she could love him? What if she did love him?

He stirred his coffee as an idea took hold. He figured he had one last chance. He was supposed to thrive on challenges, wasn't he? He'd taught himself to see challenges in a positive light and this might be his biggest challenge yet. He wasn't going to let it beat him. It wasn't over. He had one last chance and he had to take it.

Josh paced nervously in front of the lounge room fireplace. He'd spent the entire flight from Brisbane to Melbourne rehearsing what he'd say, only to arrive in Melbourne to find Georgie wasn't home. He had left Brisbane after speaking to Lou, once he'd made his decision he hadn't waited, but apparently he'd arrived on the actual day of George and Sofia's fortieth wedding anniversary and Georgie was at the hairdresser with her mother.

Despite his timing, George was pleased, but not overly surprised, to see him. Apparently he and Sofia had been discussing him and trying to work out how to entice him to Melbourne—hence the invitation to the forthcoming anniversary celebrations. His early arrival was greeted with enthusiasm, particularly when Josh explained why he'd appeared on their doorstep.

Now all that remained was to see if Georgie was similarly enthusiastic. If their chemistry was as powerful as he remembered. If she loved him like he loved her. If he could persuade her to follow her heart.

He and George heard the garage door opening, signalling the return of Georgie and her mother. George left Josh in the lounge and would send Georgie in on a pretext without alerting her to the fact that Josh was waiting.

Josh froze as he heard the doorhandle turning. He held his breath as he waited to see who was coming into the room.

Her scent reached him first.

Honey and cinnamon. It washed over him in a wave of memories.

The fireplace where he stood was on the same side of the room as the door and he knew she hadn't noticed him yet, so he took a moment just to look at her. Her tan had faded since she'd been away from the tropical Queensland sun, but her skin was still smooth and golden and her hair was still glossy and thick. It wasn't constrained but hung in a thick, straight shiny sheath over her shoulders.

She still hadn't noticed him but he'd seen her now and his feet were moving without direction from him, taking him towards her.

Georgie opened the lounge room door to retrieve her father's glasses. Movement to her left made her jump. There was someone in the room. There was someone moving towards her.

'Josh?' For a moment she wondered if her imagination was playing tricks on her. He'd been in her thoughts so much. Was she now starting to have visions? But it was him, in her parents' lounge room. His familiar gait, his familiar figure, his broad shoulders, his spiky sandy blond hair, it was definitely him.

He smiled at her and the silver flecks sparkled in his grey eyes. Her heart skipped a beat and she was halfway across the room, meeting him in the middle, halfway into his arms, before she remembered she didn't have the right to be there any more.

She stopped in her tracks. 'What are you doing here?'

She'd spent the afternoon talking about him and now he was here. In her house. This made no sense.

He didn't share her hesitation. In two strides he'd closed the remaining distance between them. 'I came to see you,' he said as he gathered her in his arms. She clung to him. It felt so good to be back in his embrace. She could feel his heart beating next to hers, echoing the rhythm.

She looked up, turning her head to him, lifting her mouth to his, and that was all it took for Josh to claim her. His lips covered hers, hungrily, passionately. There was nothing soft and gentle about this kiss. It released all the longing that had built up in the days they'd been separated. This kiss brought them home.

It left her feeling light-headed and weak-kneed and, as usual, Josh could read her thoughts. He took her hand and led her to a sofa.

'Why are you here?' Georgie couldn't remember if she'd asked him that or if he'd already told her. Her thoughts were completely chaotic and confused.

'I didn't get to say goodbye.'

'You came all the way to Melbourne to say goodbye?'

'No. I came all the way to Melbourne because I couldn't say goodbye. I don't want to say goodbye. I came to see you because there are some things I need to know.'

He was still holding her hand. His touch sent shivers of desire through her and made it impossible for her to speak. She sat beside him, mute with surprise.

He leant forward and lifted her hair in his palm, burying his face in it and inhaling deeply. Georgie closed her eyes as she felt his breath on her neck. Her heart was pounding in her chest and she could feel herself leaning in towards him, yearning for his touch. 'I remember your scent perfectly,' he said. 'And I needed to know if our chemistry was real or whether my memory has been deceiving me. Can I still read your thoughts? Do you miss me like I've missed you?'

'You've missed me?'

He nodded. 'Every minute of every day.' He reached up again and tucked her hair behind her ear. 'And I have to know, have you missed me too or has Michael made you forget all about me?'

'You know about Michael?'

Josh nodded. 'Your father told me. Does he make you happy? Is he the one for you? If he is, I'll leave now. You just have to tell me.'

His arrival had totally confused her but she did know one thing. She shook her head. 'Michael isn't for me.' This was her chance to be honest with Josh. Something had brought him to Melbourne, to her. She wanted no regrets. 'There's no spark,' she said. 'Before I met you I thought it didn't matter but now I think I need more. I want more. I want passion, excitement, exhilaration, all those things I said weren't important. I want fireworks and everything that goes with them. I want to fall in love.'

'Do you think you could love me?'

She wasn't sure she was planning on being that honest. Did Josh need to know her heart already belonged to him? She hesitated but Josh didn't wait for her reply.

'I came to ask you to marry me.'

'Marry you?' Georgie couldn't understand what was happening. She felt as though she was watching a movie of someone else's life but she'd missed the beginning. 'But you don't want to get married.'

'I didn't want to but I've changed my mind. You've changed my mind.'

Georgie was more confused than ever. 'What happened to the man who was focussing on his career? Who didn't need relationships?'

'I have the job I wanted and it's fantastic, but it's not enough. It's challenging, it's rewarding, it's keeping me busy. At the end of the day I don't want to go home, but that's not because I can't bear to leave work—it's because I don't want to go home and find that you're not there. There's more to my future than my career. You are my future. I want you. I need you.'

Georgie waited but the words she longed to hear didn't come. If he didn't love her then what was he doing here?

'Are you sure I'm not just the next challenge in your life?'

He frowned and the silver flecks in his eyes darkened to grey. 'What do you mean?'

'You thrive on challenges. You set yourself a goal and when you achieve it you need a new goal. For the past eight years that goal has been your career. Now that box is ticked. You've avoided relationships ever since Tricia died and now that your career is on track suddenly you're ready to get married?' She didn't want to be his next challenge. This wasn't what she'd been dreaming of. 'Are you sure this is what you want? Have you really thought about this?'

'This is not about Tricia,' Josh argued. 'It hasn't been about her for a long time. When she died I lost two relationships, one with her and one with my brother, and I admit it did change my view of the world. I made a decision to put my energy into my studies and my career. I wanted to concentrate on things I could have some degree of control over. I decided not to invest time and energy into relationships but that was a conscious decision. I recovered a long time ago but, until recently, I haven't had any reason to change my mind about relationships. Until I met you.

'You have opened my eyes and opened my heart. Everything has changed for me since I met you. I tried to tell myself it was Cairns affecting me, making me see things differently, but it wasn't. It was you. You showed me how to let people back into my life. I had closed myself off and you opened me up.

'The night before you left Cairns I could have made it to The Sandbar but I chose not to. I was afraid I might not be able to say goodbye. I didn't want you to go but I couldn't ask you to stay because I was afraid of what that might mean. I was scared that I might fall in love. I didn't realise I'd already fallen in love with you.'

He loved her.

'You do challenge me but you are not a challenge. You challenged the way I saw myself and you made me reassess my life. I can't ignore my feelings. I can't pretend I want to be alone any more. Everything is better when you are with me. I am better.' He got off the couch and knelt beside her on one knee. 'I want to share my life with you.' He picked up her hand. 'I know you. You exist here...' he touched their hands to his forehead '...and here...' He touched their hands to his heart. 'You're part of me,' he said as he kissed her hand. 'I love you, Georgie, and I want you to be my wife. Will you marry me?'

He loved her and he wanted her to be his wife.

But could she marry him? There was so much they'd

never discussed, so many differences. But were they big enough to stop her from having the one thing she wanted?

'What is it? What's wrong?' he asked, and she could hear the worry in his voice. She needed to find a way to make this work. He loved her and she was determined to make sure they got their hearts' desires.

'My parents—'

'Want you to be happy,' Josh interrupted. 'Your father has given us his blessing. He's told me the decision is yours.'

'He has?'

Josh nodded. 'Your father is on our side and you can let me worry about your mother.'

Georgie knew he'd have no problem there. She smiled at him. She knew exactly how her mother felt about Josh and if her parents were prepared to give their blessing she knew she could have what her heart desired. 'My mother thinks the only thing wrong with you is that you don't want to get married. Now she'll believe you're perfect.'

Josh grinned and his eyes flashed silver again. 'So that just leaves you. Do you love me?'

Georgie nodded. 'I've only ever loved you.' She never would have believed that she could love someone so completely. 'I've been waiting for you my whole life.'

'And will you marry me?'

'Do you trust me with your heart?' She had to know he could trust her to love him completely and only him. 'Do you believe I will love, honour and keep you? When I say you are the only man for me, do you know that I mean it?' She had to know that he didn't doubt her words, that he believed her promises.

Josh nodded. 'I know how you feel about your family. If you love me and if you will marry me and make me part of your family, that's all I need. You are all I need. I have faith in you and me. I trust in us.'

'And you realise what you're getting yourself into?' she asked. She had to be sure. 'A big Greek family and everything that goes along with that?'

'Why do you think we're going to live in Brisbane?' He was smiling at her but he'd never looked more serious. He held both her hands, holding her to him. 'I promise to keep a spare room ready for your family and to fly your parents up to visit whenever they want. I will immerse myself in all of it if you'll marry me.'

She had seen how he'd cared for her parents. She'd seen how he'd looked after her. She trusted him. She loved him. She belonged to him. They belonged to each other. Fate had brought them together and she knew he'd keep his promises. She knew he'd do anything for her, just as she would for him.

'I love you more than I ever imagined it was possible to love someone,' she told him. 'I will marry you. I am yours. Now and for ever.' She leant forward and kissed him, sealing their commitment, sealing their love. 'I love you now and I promise I will love you just as much on our fortieth wedding anniversary and on every one before and after.'

EPILOGUE

Josh saw his wife as she came out of the house and crossed the grass. Her hair was loose, caught behind her ear on one side with a clip, and he thought how amazing it was he never grew tired of watching her. He couldn't believe how much his life had changed in the past two years. How fortunate he was.

He crossed the lawn and went to meet her. Georgie smiled at him as she saw him approaching and his heart swelled with love and satisfaction. 'Is she asleep?'

She nodded and her hair swung in a thick, glossy curtain around her shoulders.

He slid his arm under the heavy sheath of her hair and pulled her close to him, breathing in her scent of cinnamon and honey.

'I can't believe our daughter is one year old already,' he said as he hugged her.

'I know. Soon she'll be running after her cousins and getting into all sorts of mischief.'

Josh looked over to the pool where most of Georgie's nieces and nephews were mucking about. Her parents were keeping a watchful eye on their grandchildren and her brothers and sisters-in-law were scattered around the garden, having all travelled up from Melbourne to celebrate the baby's birthday. Despite Georgie living in Brisbane, her family kept in touch and they all made a special effort to get together for big celebrations. But Josh knew that, for his daughter, seeing her cousins on an irregular basis was no match for growing up surrounded by family.

'Do you miss Melbourne or are you happy here?' he asked.

Georgie took his hand from her shoulders and held it. 'Come with me.' She smiled at him. 'I want to show you something.' She led him into the house. 'I don't miss Melbourne. Sometimes I miss my family,' she admitted, 'especially after we've had weekends like this, but I have you and I have our family.'

She opened the door to their daughter's room and led him to Alexandra's cot. Alexandra was lying on her back, arms thrown wide, spread-eagled in her favourite position, clutching one of her soft toys in her chubby fingers. Georgie stood in front of him and wrapped his arms around her waist, resting them on her stomach. 'I have everything I want right here.'

Josh rested his chin on the top of his wife's head as he watched his sleeping daughter. This was another vision he'd never grow tired of. 'What about Alexandra? Do you think we're depriving her of her cousins and grandparents?'

'She'll be okay. Don't forget, she won't know anything different,' Georgie assured him. 'We'll just have to have a big family ourselves so the kids can keep each other company.'

'More kids?' He raised an eyebrow. 'Should we start today?' he asked with a grin.

Georgie laughed. 'We've already started,' she said as she squeezed his fingers and turned her head to smile at him. 'I'm nine weeks pregnant.'

'What? You are?'

Georgie nodded. She'd planned to tell him the news when her family had all returned to Melbourne as she'd wanted it to be just between them for a while, but once she'd had a positive pregnancy test she'd found it very difficult to keep the news from Josh. She knew that if she didn't tell him soon, he'd guess. His ability to read her thoughts hadn't diminished since they'd married but, for once, if the stunned look on his face was anything to go by, she'd managed to surprise him this time. 'Is that okay? Not too much to deal with?'

'Are you kidding?' His eyes were shining silver and he was grinning like the Cheshire cat. 'Being married to you, being a father, has been the best thing that's ever happened to me. Adding to our family can only make things better,' he said as he smoothed his fingers over her stomach. 'It's fantastic news.'

The gentle pressure of his fingers sent a shiver of desire through Georgie. She'd never imagined she could love someone so completely. She turned to face him, careful to stay within his embrace. 'I love you. Thank you for sharing your life with me.'

'Our life together is still only just beginning,' he said as he bent his head and kissed her softly on the lips. 'I am going to love you for ever.'

And as he claimed her lips a second time there was not a trace of doubt in her mind that he would do just that. She had everything she'd ever wished for.

* * * * *

Mills & Boon® Hardback

April 2012

ROMANCE

HISTORICAL

MEDICAL

Mills & Boon® Large Print

April 2012

ROMANCE

Jewel in His Crown	Lynne Graham
The Man Every Woman Wants	Miranda Lee
Once a Ferrara Wife...	Sarah Morgan
Not Fit for a King?	Jane Porter
Snowbound with Her Hero	Rebecca Winters
Flirting with Italian	Liz Fielding
Firefighter Under the Mistletoe	Melissa McClone
The Tycoon Who Healed Her Heart	Melissa James

HISTORICAL

The Lady Forfeits	Carole Mortimer
Valiant Soldier, Beautiful Enemy	Diane Gaston
Winning the War Hero's Heart	Mary Nichols
Hostage Bride	Anne Herries

MEDICAL

Breaking Her No-Dates Rule	Emily Forbes
Waking Up With Dr Off-Limits	Amy Andrews
Tempted by Dr Daisy	Caroline Anderson
The Fiancée He Can't Forget	Caroline Anderson
A Cotswold Christmas Bride	Joanna Neil
All She Wants For Christmas	Annie Claydon

0312 GEN STD LP

Mills & Boon® Hardback

May 2012

ROMANCE

A Vow of Obligation	Lynne Graham
Defying Drakon	Carole Mortimer
Playing the Greek's Game	Sharon Kendrick
One Night in Paradise	Maisey Yates
His Majesty's Mistake	Jane Porter
Duty and the Beast	Trish Morey
The Darkest of Secrets	Kate Hewitt
Behind the Castello Doors	Chantelle Shaw
The Morning After The Wedding Before	Anne Oliver
Never Stay Past Midnight	Mira Lyn Kelly
Valtieri's Bride	Caroline Anderson
Taming the Lost Prince	Raye Morgan
The Nanny Who Kissed Her Boss	Barbara McMahon
Falling for Mr Mysterious	Barbara Hannay
One Day to Find a Husband	Shirley Jump
The Last Woman He'd Ever Date	Liz Fielding
Sydney Harbour Hospital: Lexi's Secret	Melanie Milburne
West Wing to Maternity Wing!	Scarlet Wilson

HISTORICAL

Lady Priscilla's Shameful Secret	Christine Merrill
Rake with a Frozen Heart	Marguerite Kaye
Miss Cameron's Fall from Grace	Helen Dickson
Society's Most Scandalous Rake	Isabelle Goddard

MEDICAL

Diamond Ring for the Ice Queen	Lucy Clark
No.1 Dad in Texas	Dianne Drake
The Dangers of Dating Your Boss	Sue MacKay
The Doctor, His Daughter and Me	Leonie Knight

Mills & Boon® Large Print
May 2012

ROMANCE

The Man Who Risked It All	Michelle Reid
The Sheikh's Undoing	Sharon Kendrick
The End of her Innocence	Sara Craven
The Talk of Hollywood	Carole Mortimer
Master of the Outback	Margaret Way
Their Miracle Twins	Nikki Logan
Runaway Bride	Barbara Hannay
We'll Always Have Paris	Jessica Hart

HISTORICAL

The Lady Confesses	Carole Mortimer
The Dangerous Lord Darrington	Sarah Mallory
The Unconventional Maiden	June Francis
Her Battle-Scarred Knight	Meriel Fuller

MEDICAL

The Child Who Rescued Christmas	Jessica Matthews
Firefighter With A Frozen Heart	Dianne Drake
Mistletoe, Midwife...Miracle Baby	Anne Fraser
How to Save a Marriage in a Million	Leonie Knight
Swallowbrook's Winter Bride	Abigail Gordon
Dynamite Doc or Christmas Dad?	Marion Lennox